Be Afraid of the Dark

Noise. Just a hint of it. And movement. Slow and surreptitious.

Some son of a bitch was in the room.

Longarm's eyes opened wide, but he could see nothing. The lamps had been extinguished, and the place was as dark as the inside of a whore's heart.

Someone was creeping up on him.

Longarm reached for his Colt but it was gone. He lay there wearing only his damned underwear. He had no idea when the woman had stripped him, probably to make him more comfortable. Now he might have to pay for that comfort with his life. He had no gun, no knife, and was far from his best physically after the blow to the head he'd taken earlier.

But he was damned well not going to just lie there like a rabbit waiting for the wolf.

Longarm moved very cautiously, not wanting to cause the cot ropes to creak. He gathered himself and listened closely, trying his damnedest to gauge exactly where the intruder was.

He had to be right. He would have only one chance. If he blew that, he might as well just crawl into a coffin and ask them to start nailing it shut.

But, by damn, he did have that one chance . . .

DON'T MISS THESE
ALL-ACTION WESTERN SERIES
FROM THE BERKLEY PUBLISHING GROUP

***THE GUNSMITH** by J. R. Roberts*

Clint Adams was a legend among lawmen, outlaws, and ladies. They called him . . . the Gunsmith.

***LONGARM** by Tabor Evans*

The popular long-running series about Deputy U.S. Marshal Long—his life, his loves, his fight for justice.

***SLOCUM** by Jake Logan*

Today's longest-running action Western. John Slocum rides a deadly trail of hot blood and cold steel.

***BUSHWHACKERS** by B. J. Lanagan*

An action-packed series by the creators of Longarm! The rousing adventures of the most brutal gang of cutthroats ever assembled—Quantrill's Raiders.

***DIAMONDBACK** by Guy Brewer*

Dex Yancey is Diamondback, a Southern gentleman turned con man when his brother cheats him out of the family fortune. Ladies love him. Gamblers hate him. But nobody pulls one over on Dex . . .

***WILDGUN** by Jack Hanson*

The blazing adventures of mountain man Will Barlow—from the creators of Longarm!

***TEXAS TRACKER** by Tom Calhoun*

Meet J.T. Law: the most relentless—and dangerous—manhunter in all Texas. Where sheriffs and posses fail, he's the best man to bring in the most vicious outlaws—for a price.

TABOR EVANS

LONGARM

MEETS
BLACKBEARD

JOVE BOOKS, NEW YORK

THE BERKLEY PUBLISHING GROUP
Published by the Penguin Group
Penguin Group (USA) Inc.
375 Hudson Street, New York, New York 10014, USA
Penguin Group (Canada), 90 Eglinton Avenue East, Suite 700, Toronto, Ontario M4P 2Y3, Canada
(a division of Pearson Penguin Canada Inc.)
Penguin Books Ltd., 80 Strand, London WC2R 0RL, England
Penguin Group Ireland, 25 St. Stephen's Green, Dublin 2, Ireland (a division of Penguin Books Ltd.)
Penguin Group (Australia), 250 Camberwell Road, Camberwell, Victoria 3124, Australia
(a division of Pearson Australia Group Pty. Ltd.)
Penguin Books India Pvt. Ltd., 11 Community Centre, Panchsheel Park, New Delhi—110 017, India
Penguin Group (NZ), 67 Apollo Drive, Rosedale, North Shore 0745, Auckland, New Zealand
(a division of Pearson New Zealand Ltd.)
Penguin Books (South Africa) (Pty.) Ltd., 24 Sturdee Avenue, Rosebank, Johannesburg 2196,
South Africa

Penguin Books Ltd., Registered Offices: 80 Strand, London WC2R 0RL, England

This is a work of fiction. Names, characters, places, and incidents either are the product of the author's imagination or are used fictitiously, and any resemblance to actual persons, living or dead, business establishments, events, or locales is entirely coincidental.

LONGARM MEETS BLACKBEARD

A Jove Book / published by arrangement with the author

PRINTING HISTORY
Jove edition / July 2007

Copyright © 2007 by The Berkley Publishing Group.

ISBN: 978-0-515-14322-5

JOVE®
Jove Books are published by The Berkley Publishing Group,
a division of Penguin Group (USA) Inc.,
375 Hudson Street, New York, New York 10014.
JOVE is a registered trademark of Penguin Group (USA) Inc.
The "J" design is a trademark belonging to Penguin Group (USA) Inc.

PRINTED IN THE UNITED STATES OF AMERICA

10 9 8 7 6 5 4 3 2 1

Chapter 1

He heard the *snickety-clack* of a revolver being cocked and saw what looked like a pistol barrel poking around the corner of the building he was approaching.

Custis Long threw himself down, his hand streaking for his .44 Colt while he was still flat out in the air. He hit hard and rolled violently to his left as a pistol boomed and white gun smoke blossomed. The slug sizzled close above his right shoulder, ricocheted off the sunbaked ground, and went whining off into the distance.

Longarm braced his wrist with his left hand, took careful aim, and waited half a heartbeat.

The son of a bitch around the corner leaned out to take another shot or perhaps to see if the first one had found its mark. As soon as Longarm had a target, he triggered his Colt.

The big .44 bucked in his hand and a wet, red dimple appeared on the man's forehead just left of center. His head suddenly changed shape, his hat popped off, and a pink spray of blood and brain created a halo in the air behind him.

Longarm rolled again, to the right this time, and came to his knees.

There. Another gun barrel. A rifle. This shooter was more timid than the first had been and was pressed tightly against the side wall of the hardware store across the street. He was young and he looked frightened. But then he had just seen his twin brother's brains blown out of the back of the asshole's skull.

"Drop it!"

Instead, the idiot kid took a deep breath and stepped forward with the rifle cocked and leveled.

Longarm fired again and rolled left. Aimed and fired—fast noises don't do shit—and saw dust puff off the kid's shirt front.

"Dammit."

Longarm rose to his knees, Colt held ready, and watched the young man topple facedown onto the boards of the hardware store's sidewalk. He hit hard, the sound dull, and did not try to brace himself when he hit. He bounced. When they hit like that they are no longer a threat.

The man who had just taken two lives stood and looked warily around. After all, the Benton brothers could have found some friends here.

There seemed to be no immediate threat so he moved back against the wall of a hattery, flipped the loading gate of his Colt open, and quickly thumbed fresh cartridges into the weapon.

The street, which one minute earlier had been busy with commerce and voices and the rumble of wagons, was eerily silent now, the people of the community suddenly invisible. Sensibly invisible if the truth be told. A man who dies from an unintended bullet is just as dead as the son of a bitch who is shot down on purpose.

Longarm finished reloading and shoved his Colt back into the cross-draw holster that rode high on his belly just to the left of his belt buckle.

Only when he was satisfied that the revolver was properly holstered did he lean down to brush the red dust off his brown corduroy trousers, calfskin vest, and the elbows of his brown tweed coat.

He was a tall man, lean and craggy, with sun wrinkles at the corners of his eyes. He had dark brown hair and a huge sweep of handlebar mustache. His eyes were a soft golden brown, although they could appear to be cold steel to anyone fool enough to stand against him.

He wore a flat-crowned brown Stetson, a black gun belt rigged for a cross-draw, and black stovepipe boots with low cavalry heels suitable for walking.

Experience had taught him what to do next. He reached inside his coat and extracted his wallet, then flipped it open to display the badge of a deputy United States marshal. He waited.

A minute, no more, and he heard running footsteps that slowed to a cautious walk before they reached the mouth of the alley beside the hattery. The man who stepped into view was carrying a shotgun held at waist level. He was middle-aged and graying and looked like a man who just might know what to do with a shooter like that one. He also had a small nickel-plated badge pinned to his vest.

"Deputy U.S. marshal," Longarm announced himself, holding his own badge in plain view.

The local lawman blinked twice and looked suspiciously from Frank to Tommy Benton and back again. Both were facedown on the ground, Tommy in a large and still spreading pool of his own blood and Frank

3

with the back of his head blown apart like an overripe watermelon dropped off the back of a wagon.

"Who . . . what . . . ?"

Longarm introduced himself and ambled over to stand beside the local. People began to show themselves on the street again.

"Long, eh? I've heard of you." The man lowered the hammers on his scattergun and draped it over his forearm. "I'm Ben Waters. I'm the town marshal."

"Pleasure t' meet you, Marshal Waters."

"Call me Ben."

"And I'm Longarm."

"So what's the deal with these two?" Waters asked.

"This one is Frank Benton. That one over there is his brother, Tommy. The two of them got hard up for money or maybe just bored and they decided to spice up their lives some. They robbed a jeweler in Silverthorne an' took off runnin'. Sold what they stole to a man in Fairplay. They didn't have any idea about the value of what they had. Sold it dirt cheap.

"Their mistake was selling to an honest man. When he heard about the robbery, he put two an' two together an' wired my boss down in Denver. That was three weeks ago an' I've been on their tails ever since." Longarm sighed. "I sure woulda rather taken them in in 'cuffs than in a box. They was only eighteen, nineteen years old, something like that."

"They won't get any older now," Ben Waters said.

"No, an' that's fair enough. They had their choices to make an' they did a lousy job of it. What bothers me is that these boys got folks back there somewhere. What they done to their ma and pa was the poorest choice of all."

"I don't mean to be crass or unfeeling, Longarm, but

we don't have a budget to pay for burying strangers. Do you?"

"Not exactly. Tell you what, Marshal. I'll send a wire . . . . You got the telegraph here, don't you?"

"Yes, of course." Waters seemed mildly offended that anyone would doubt the modernity of his town.

"Fine. I'll wire my boss to tell him what's happened. He can notify the boys' folks about where they are an' let the family decide what they want done. How's that sound?"

"Fine. And when you're done getting that wire off maybe you would join me for a drink. The telegraph office is right there on your right. It's inside the stage station. I'll see to having these bodies collected, then I'll be across the street at the Blue Bull saloon. I'd be proud to buy you a drink when you have a few minutes free."

"Which I surely will while I'm waiting to hear back from Marshal Vail. Reckon I can take you up on that offer, Ben, and I thank you."

The town marshal nodded and strode away, motioning for the locals to quit gawking at the blood and the gore and go on about their business.

Chapter 2

Longarm yawned and reached inside his coat for a cheroot, bit the twist off, and spat it into his hand, then dropped the stub of dark tobacco into an ashtray on the table before him. He lit the slender cigar and stretched, crossing his boots at the ankles.

"I hope this marshal of yours will authorize the use of federal funds for the burials. We just don't have money for this sort of thing," Ben Waters complained.

"I done what you asked," Longarm told him. "I got that wire off. All I can do now is t' wait for Billy to respond." He shook his head and took a moment to puff on the cheroot. "Nothing else I can do till I hear back from him."

"You just don't understand. The cemetery is privately owned. The town has to pay for any plots that are used. Five dollars each. Then there is the cost of the embalming, the laying out, the coffin itself . . . The total comes to almost fifteen dollars for each indigent who is buried out there. I know, because we had some sort of flu last year. More than a dozen people died, some of them complete strangers, and we're still paying off those expenses. Our town budget . . ."

Longarm was more than a little weary of hearing about the Grandview, Nevada, town budget. And where did they come up with a name like that anyway. Grand view? Bullshit. There was nothing but rock and sand for miles in any direction.

Of course there was mineral down below, and all that rock and sand was owned by someone. But . . . shit! He was tired of hearing Ben Waters talk about it.

Longarm gathered his feet under him, stuck the cheroot in the corner of his mouth, and stood. "I'm gonna go take a walk," he said.

"What? Oh." Waters waved his hand dismissively. "Go on then. It isn't your problem. Just shoot them down and leave them lying there, right? Let someone else clean up your mess."

"You are startin' to piss me off, Ben."

"Fine. So shoot me. The town can pay for my burial too."

Obviously the town marshal was in no mood to listen to reason and too much in the mood for an argument. Longarm turned and got the hell out of there without another word.

He left the saloon and headed down the street. It was much too soon to expect a response to that telegram from Billy, and he certainly did not want to return to the Blue Bull and Marshal Ben Waters's bellyaching. It was the middle of the afternoon and well short of the dinner hour. He was not particularly hungry, but there was a café half a block ahead and he had nothing better to do. He altered direction and headed for it.

"Hello? Is anybody here?" The café door was unlocked and a little sign propped in the front window read OPEN but there were neither customers nor cooks in evidence inside. Longarm removed his hat and stood by the door. After a moment a woman poked her head out of what he assumed was a storeroom. The kitchen occupied the left wall of the place, separated from the customers only by a low counter lined with stools. "Did you call, sir?"

"I was wonderin' if you're open for business."

"Yes. Of course."

Longarm helped himself to one of the stools at the counter, and the woman stepped into the room. She went to a basin of water on a stand near the side door and very meticulously washed her hands with soft lye soap, then dried them with a scrap of flour sacking.

Longarm managed to keep from falling off his stool, it was hard not to. He struggled to not show it but inside he was laughing fit to bust. When she had turned away from him to wash her hands, it became obvious where this woman had just been. The back of her dress was tucked up, the hem caught inside the waist of her drawers. Obviously she didn't know it, but from the back she was pretty thoroughly exposed.

She was not a pretty woman, long in the face with mousy brown hair. But she sure did have a tidy butt and long, lean legs. Longarm guessed her age to be reaching toward the upper end of her thirties.

Mighty nice legs, yes, sir. He choked back an impulse to guffaw and managed to sit there prim and polite while the woman very carefully washed before turning to him. "How can I help you, sir?"

"Coffee would be good," he said. "Maybe some ham, eggs, fried taters."

"I have not seen a chicken since I came to this godforsaken country, and the only ham I have is so salty it would pucker your mouth and pull your mustache inside."

"You do manage t' make things sound appetizing," Longarm told her.

She smiled. "At least I'm honest."

"Yes, ma'am."

"I could offer you antelope steak and those fried potatoes," she suggested.

"Sounds like just what I was wantin'."

She turned away. The dress had not yet fallen loose from her drawers, which were rather puffy and had tiny pink ribbons sewed on to them. He did like the view though. A Grandview indeed. At that thought he almost burst out laughing but again managed to choke it down.

The lady took her time lifting an iron plate off the stovetop so she could drop in some chunks of coal, then set a skillet of grease on to heat while she sliced a steak off what was left of an antelope haunch. She had potatoes already peeled and sliced and soaking in a pot of water. As soon as the grease was hot enough, she flopped the steak in and surrounded it with potatoes and some sliced onion. The aroma coming from that skillet was almost enough to take Longarm's mind off the shape of her legs and the sight of that rucked-up dress. Almost.

It was an . . . interesting meal to say the least.

But he got through it, then paid, leaving only a modest tip. Anything larger might be misinterpreted once this lady discovered the show she had staged for him.

He kinda wished he could still be there when that discovery was made, but common sense and a strong inclination toward self-preservation sent him out the door before that happened.

Chapter 3

"Dealer opens for a penny."

"I'll see that."

"Call."

It was only a penny but . . . fuck it . . . the cards were cold this evening. Longarm tossed his hand into the middle of the table—stinking, lousy cards every one of them—and stood, reaching for what remained of a cheroot. "I'm out, gents. I thank you for the game." He touched the brim of his Stetson and ambled out into the cool night air and down the block to the next saloon.

This one seemed to cater to workingmen. The walls were bare and there were no tables or chairs, just a long bar with a brass rail and tin cuspidors. There was no mirror, which was likely an indicator or what sort of place this was.

A couple of bedraggled whores, Mexican or maybe Indian, looked up when he came in but quickly scowled in Longarm's direction when it became apparent that he had no interest in them.

Longarm propped his elbows on the bar and waited for the gent in the greasy apron to come by.

"Whiskey or beer, what'll it be?"

"Got any rye whiskey?"

"You can call it that if you like. Or call it Henrietta if that pleases you more."

"I'll have the whiskey, thank you."

"You'll be sorry." The barkeep poured from a crockery jug and pushed the tin cup in front of Longarm.

"Jesus!" Longarm blurted after the first taste. "This is awful." Obviously the shit was cobbled up out of raw alcohol, gunpowder, pepper, and God knew what else.

"I told ya. You want another?"

"No. Gimme a beer."

"You don't want the rest of that red-eye?"

"Not likely."

The bartender took Longarm's mug and very carefully returned the rotgut to the crockery jug, then filled the same mug to the brim with a flat, watery beer drawn from a keg at the end of the counter.

"I got to charge you for both," he said when he pushed the mug back down the bar to Longarm.

"Got to?"

"All right, maybe I don't *got* to. But I'm going to. Is that better?"

"You took your whiskey back."

"You drank part of it." The man pulled the mug of beer back toward his side of the bar, ready to take it back too if the customer didn't pay. Longarm got the impression this was not a unique experience in this joint. "Now pay up or I'll call the marshal."

That was threat enough. Longarm quickly dragged a quarter out of his pocket and laid it down. If there was anything he did not want this evening it was to have to listen to Ben Waters bellyache all over again about the town budget.

The barkeep snatched the quarter away almost before Longarm put it down. There was no change offered.

And the beer was almost as bad as the whiskey had been. At least the flavor of the one washed away the foul taste of the other.

"Refill?" the bartender asked a couple minutes later.

"Sure. I got nothing better to do."

And that, sadly, was the natural truth.

The big man was crowding him. Deliberately so, Longarm thought. There was more than enough room at the bar for everyone who was present and a half dozen more if need be. But this fellow stood close enough to Longarm to bump his elbow whenever Longarm tried to raise his mug for a drink. It was not jostling exactly, just . . . contact. Very unwelcome contact.

Longarm moved a few inches aside, giving way to the rude son of a bitch. The big fellow moved with him.

Longarm turned around, presenting his back to the man. The asshole moved around in front of Longarm, pushing another gent aside, taking his place so that once again he was face-to-face with Longarm. And this time he was more nose-to-nose and belly-to-belly.

The man was burly and deeply tanned, obviously someone who worked outdoors and very likely someone who did physical labor because his muscles bulged to the point of straining the sleeves of his shirt.

He had dark hair, a thick mat of it curling over the top of his shirt. And quite a bit of it sticking out of his nostrils too.

He was not wearing a gun and did not appear to be carrying a knife either.

Longarm sighed. But what the hell. . . . "What're you doin', mister, growing out your nose hair 'til you can braid 'em an' toss 'em over your shoulder like that continental soldier everybody sings about?"

"Huh?"

"Never mind," Longarm said, raising his mug toward the fellow in a silently mocking salute.

"I know who you are," the fellow said.

"I have no idea who you are. And I really don't care either." Longarm set the mug down. He did not think he was going to hang on to it for just a little while here.

"You think I oughta be scared of you 'cause you killed them two guys today."

"No," Longarm said with a hint of smile. "I think you ought t' be scared because if I take the notion to, I'll beat the living shit outa you, asshole."

"Did you call me . . . *oof!*" The rest of the sentence was cut off when Longarm's fist landed in the big man's breadbasket, driving the breath out of him and dropping him to one knee.

With most men the fight would have ended right there. This one dropped his head for a moment, then shook himself like an old mossback bull accepting the challenge of another.

Then he came up swinging. He caught Longarm with a wild roundhouse left that rang Longarm's bell. It numbed the entire right side of his head and put a buzzing in his right ear. This guy might not know much about the sweet science of fighting but he damned sure knew how to punch, and he had some pepper on it.

Longarm backed away—funny thing how he had plenty of room now, the other patrons no longer crowding close—and lifted his dukes, bobbing and swaying to give himself time to gather his wits from wherever it was they'd flown off to.

The man thought he had Longarm in trouble—not

that he was all that wrong about it—and moved in as if for a finishing blow. Longarm was not as far out of it as the fellow seemed to think though. As soon as he came within range, Longarm tagged him with a jab that was hard enough to pulp the fellow's nose and send a flow of blood into that mat of curly hair on his chest.

This time the guy was ready for it. He threw another of those wild lefts, which Longarm easily ducked under.

Oh, shit! The left merely served to set him up, and did it ever. The man followed that roundhouse left with a brutally hard underhand right that landed flush on its target and blew out Longarm's lamp.

Birdies sang and bells rang, and it was good night, sweet prince.

Chapter 4

Longarm blinked. It was bright. Too damned bright. It hurt his eyes and made his head ache something ferocious. "Wha . . . ?"

"Shh. Lie still now." The voice was that of a woman but he could not see who she was because of a halo of brightness behind her head. Her face was in shadows.

Not for a single damn moment did Custis Long suspect she was an angel or that he had died and gone to heaven. He knew better than that. When he went, he fully expected to go in the other direction. But meanwhile he would have a helluva good time.

This only confused him. He blinked again and screwed his face into a fright mask, trying to cut down on the brightness.

"Be still, I told you." This time the voice that had been tender held a sharp edge. Longarm lay still. Very. He quit worrying about the light and shut his eyes.

She touched a spot on his forehead that made his eyes snap open again, and he jerked so hard in response that he came halfway up into a sitting position.

"I'm sorry. I'm trying to clean you up a little. You have a goose egg the size of Jacob's fist."

"Ja . . ." He paused, swallowed, tried again. "Jacob?"

She raised a cool, damp washcloth and bathed his face and forehead with it, speaking as she did so. She smelled of yeast and bacon grease, and he finally remembered who she was. The woman at the café. He should have seen that immediately, but his thoughts were more than a little muddled at the moment.

"Jacob is the man who hit you. He is the one who brought you to me." She laughed softly. "Everyone in town knows that I am the one who takes in the birds with the broken wings."

"Why?"

"Why what?"

"Why'd Ja . . . him. Why'd he help?"

"Jacob loves to fight but no one in Grandview will fight him anymore. He always wins. The marshal told him to stop beating up on people or he would have to face charges of public disturbance and serve ninety days in jail."

The amount of time sounded excessive to Longarm. But then he did not know the local justice of the peace either. Could be the man was a real firecracker. Or that Jacob had been in trouble just about once too often already.

"Anyway, Jacob was afraid you were really hurt, so he picked you up and carried you to me."

"Carried?"

"Jacob is an unusually strong man."

"Lordy, I reckon he is. That washrag o' yours feels almighty good, ma'am."

She smiled. "I will take that as a hint." She turned away, dipped the cloth into a basin of cool water and

wrung it out before applying it to his face and his forehead again. It felt wonderful.

"Where was I?" she mused aloud while she bathed his
face. "Oh, yes. Jacob. He brought you in and begged me to
take care of you." She laughed. It was a nice sound, soft
and gentle. "And to *not* tell Ben. Ben is our town marshal.
He . . ."

"I know him."

"Do you? Good. So does Jacob though. All too well.
He was hoping Ben wouldn't hear about him fighting
again." She shrugged. "Fat chance of that. By now Ben
will have heard every detail and likely a lot of embel-
lishment too."

Longarm tried to sit up.

"Now you lie still. You are in no shape to be up and
walking. Not just yet." She pressed a hand against his
chest and, light though her touch was, it was too much
for him to overcome. He was still deeper under the in-
fluence of that punch than he'd realized.

"I have to get a message to Marshal Waters."

"I can do that for you if you like. What is it?"

"Tell . . ." Longarm licked his dry lips and took a
breath before he tried again. "Tell Ben that I'm the one
who threw the first punch."

"Did you really?"

"Uh-huh. The guy was crowding me an' I got pi—
angry. But yeah, I threw the first punch. Jacob shouldn't
get in trouble for what I done. I want Waters t' know
that. Can you tell him for me, please?"

"Does it have to be tonight?"

"If it wouldn't be no bother, ma'am. I'd hate for your
friend Jacob t' spend the night in the pokey on account
o' something I done."

The woman sat back and gave him a quizzical look.

19

Then she nodded. "All right. Lie back and close your eyes. I can turn the lamps down now. You seem clean enough for the time being. Go to sleep if you can. I'll step out and look for Ben. He should be somewhere on the street making his night rounds about now. I'll be back soon."

"Thank you."

He felt the bed sway a little and heard the creak of rope springs when she stood. Once she turned the wicks down on the lamps he could see better. He was lying in a small room with board and batten walls, the one narrow cot where he was at the moment, a washstand, and, on a shelf beneath the washbasin, a covered chamber pot. That was something he needed, either that or an outhouse, but he was in no shape to sit up unassisted much less go walking somewhere. It would just have to wait.

"I won't be but a few minutes."

"Thank you," he said again.

The café proprietor—proprietress?—left the room. The café, he could see when she opened the door, was dark now, closed for the night. He wondered how long he had been here.

Not that he needed to worry about that right now. He was not going anywhere until his head stopped spinning.

He shut his eyes again and felt himself drifting away on a soft and puffy cloud.

Chapter 5

Noise. Just a hint of it. And movement. Slow and surreptitious. A floorboard creaked and he heard a faint swish of cloth rubbing against cloth.

Some son of a bitch was in the room.

Longarm's eyes opened wide but he could see nothing. The lamps had been extinguished, and the place was as black as the inside of a whore's heart.

He could . . . feel more than anything.

Someone was creeping up on him.

Longarm reached for his Colt but it was gone. He lay there wearing only his damned underwear. He had no idea when the woman had stripped him. Making him more comfortable, he supposed. Now he might have to pay for that comfort with his life. He had no gun, no knife, and was far from his best physically after the blow to the head he'd taken earlier.

But he was not—he damned well was *not*—going to just lie there like a rabbit waiting for the wolf.

Fuck that!

Longarm moved very cautiously, not wanting to cause the cot ropes to creak. He gathered himself and listened closely, trying his damnedest to gauge exactly where the intruder was.

He had to be right. He would have only one chance. If he blew that, he might as well just crawl into a coffin and ask them to start nailing it shut.

But, by damn, he *did* have that one chance.

He heard a very soft and muffled *clink*. Crockery, it sounded like. Shit, yes. The washbasin. That was where the intruder was. Right . . . over . . . there.

Longarm came off the bed like a tightly wound spring let suddenly loose, and came up with a roar.

He hit the bastard hard and carried him down to the floor, winding up on top of him, pinning him hard.

Longarm was still woozy and weak but he could still . . .

The intruder smelled of yeast. And grease. And wood smoke.

And the body that lay beneath him was soft and yielding. Rather pleasantly soft.

"Oh, shit."

"I startled you," the woman said. "I'm sorry."

"Christ, I'm in your home. I'm takin' up your bed. And now you're apologizin' for comin' into your own home? Ma'am, I'm the one has t' be sorry, ungrateful son of a bitch that I am."

"I only came in to use the thunder mug. I should have gone down the alley. There are some outhouses down there. I just hate to go out at night. A woman alone. You understand, I hope."

"O' course I do. Really, ma'am, I apologize for what I've done here."

Now that he was fully awake and realized what was happening he became aware that the skirts of her dress were hiked up to her waist. Either she'd already used the

22

receptacle or she was just about to when Longarm jumped her. Her legs and belly were bare. And soft.

He also realized to his considerable embarrassment that he was now lying on top of her and between her legs as if . . . oh, shit!

Worse, his body knew what he was lying against before he did and now he had a hard-on he could use to drill rock.

She had to be able to feel it there. So did he. Now.

"Sorry. Sorry." He gathered himself to pick himself up and back away but the woman stopped him.

"You don't have to get up. To tell you the truth it's nice to feel a man there again. It has been . . . a long time."

" 'Zat so?"

"Yes, it is. I'm what they call a grass widow. My man walked out just over two years ago."

"I'm real sorry t' hear that."

"Don't be. Pete was one mean, miserable son of a bitch. He was crude and hairy and he never bathed more than once a month. He was a drunk and a wife beater and I hated his rotten guts. But he had a hard dick, and I liked that well enough. It is the only thing about Pete that I miss, and I miss it plenty. I haven't been with a man since Pete left. I don't want to let any of the men around here into my bed. I know good and well they would think it was license to order me around if they ever once had a piece of what I've got. But you . . . that is an uncommonly fine dick you've got your own self there, Marshal."

"You know who I am then," he said.

"Yes. Ben Waters told me when I passed your message along."

"Mes— Oh, yeah, that." He grinned, never mind that

it was too dark to read facial expressions. Most can be heard in a person's tone of voice anyway. "Ma'am, I either gotta get up off o' you or else put that blind snake where it wants t' go."

She lifted her butt and spread her thighs wide apart.

"Reckon that's answer enough," he said, pulling himself loose from his underwear.

He backed off just far enough to let the head of his cock hang free between them. He felt her hand fumble between their bodies, find his shaft, and guide him down and forward until he plunged deep into the honey pot.

"Hard," she whispered. "I like it hard."

"Yes, ma'am," he said. "Hard is how you're gonna get it."

Chapter 6

She was a wild ride. She bucked and thrashed like a filly carrying its first saddle, like she was trying to bruise his belly by pounding it with her own.

It was not a ride Longarm objected to taking. He met her stroke for pile-driving stroke until both of them exploded into gasping, shuddering climaxes.

"God," she whispered, clinging to him with her arms and her legs alike. "That was . . . powerful."

"Yeah. I couldn't agree more," Longarm mumbled. He stayed where he was long enough to catch his breath, then rolled off her. The floorboards were cold and gritty under his bare ass. Not that he was complaining.

"Are you feeling better now?" she asked, reaching up to very gently touch his forehead. Her touch, light though it was, made him wince. "I think that goose egg is going down a little. Help me up, will you? I think we should move to the bed." It was too dark in the room for him to see her facial expression but the timbre of her voice suggested that she was smiling. "I have some thoughts about what we can do next. If you are up to it, that is."

"I'll try an' bear up under the strain," Longarm said in a dry, drawn-out drawl.

And indeed he was *up* to it.

"Mmmph!" He took a deep breath. His mouth tasted like a buffalo wallow smells. "What're you doin', woman?"

"Getting up, of course."

"What the hell time z'it?"

She was sitting on the side of the bed, leaning over. Probably putting on stockings or shoes. "Four o'clock."

"Good Lord, we only got to sleep an hour or so ago."

"Even so, I have dough to set and hotcake batter to mix and coffee to boil. Don't forget, I'll have customers in here expecting their breakfasts at six."

"You open at six?"

"Every day of my life."

"Remind me t' not open a café when I retire someday. If I live that long."

"Don't joke about things like that."

"Sorry. I wouldn't of thought you'd care."

"Of course I care. I like you." She stood up and crossed the room. By the sound he could tell she had her shoes on, ready to go to work.

"Well I like you too. But I'm not getting up at no damn four in the morning. Not when I don't got no reason to. Unless you need me t' help you with somethin'."

"Stay here as long as you like, but when you do get up I would appreciate it if you would slip out the back and come around to the front to get your breakfast. I don't want to get tongues to wagging, if you know what I mean."

"Uh-huh. Small towns an' gossip always go together just fine."

He could hear the smile in her voice again when she said, "When you're ready I'll fix you a special breakfast. We'll want to build up your strength."

"Does that mean I've been invited back here after you close tonight?"

"Yes. If . . . if you want to, that is."

"I want to. I'm waitin' for a wire from my boss, but if I'm still in Grandview you can count on me comin' back for seconds. Or . . . what would it be, d'you figure?"

She giggled. "Tonight would be for fifths, I think. Or sixths. Something lovely like that."

"Make that breakfast a big one then 'cause I'm gonna need my strength."

She returned to the bed, leaned down, and lightly kissed him. "I will see you later, Custis." Then she was gone. The deep darkness in the room lessened just a bit when she opened the door that led into her café. Then he heard the solid *clunk* of the door closing.

Longarm stretched out—the bed had been mighty crowded when there were two of them sharing it—and closed his eyes for some more much-needed sleep.

Chapter 7

Longarm finished his meal—big? it had damned well been huge, and now his belly was so full it ached—and laid a silver dollar down beside his plate. The lady glanced around to make sure no one was listening, then whispered, "You needn't do that, you know."

"Do what?"

Her eyes shifted toward the dollar. "That. I mean . . . you don't have to pay."

"I ate, didn't I? This is a café, ain't it? Of course I'm gonna pay." He grinned. "Or anyway the government is. I'll put it down on my expense account when I get back t' Denver. Besides, it's only fair."

"Just as long as it isn't . . . uh . . ."

"Payment for services rendered? Not damn likely." The grin became wider. "If it was for that, lady, I'd have t' come up with a helluva lot more than a poor deputy can afford."

She began to blush. "You're just saying that."

"I am sayin' it. 'Cause I mean it."

"You do know how to turn a girl's head. And . . . other things too."

Longarm laughed and leaned back from the counter. The front door opened and a kid of fourteen or so came in. Instead of finding a seat at one of the few available tables he looked around, then marched straight to Longarm. "Would you be Marshal Long, sir?" The boy's face was flushed, and he was out of breath, obviously from running.

"That's me. What can I do for you?"

"I have a telegram for you, sir." The kid reached deep inside his pants pocket and pulled out a crumpled yellow flimsy. "This came in overnight, sir, but I just now come on duty. An' I didn't know where you was. I been all over town looking for you. I hope that's all right."

"I hope it is too, but I won't really know that until I read it. Whatever it says, you got it here the quickest you could." Longarm reached into his pocket and pulled out a dime to tip the kid even though a nickel or even a three-cent piece would have been adequate. "Here. You did good."

The boy's eyes widened, and he smiled. "Thank you, sir. Thanks a lot." He turned and raced back out, allowing the café door to slam shut behind him.

Chuckling, and perhaps reminiscing a little over the youthful display of boundless energy, Longarm unfolded the telegram.

NO INSTRUCTION YET RE BENTON BROZ STOP MAY HAVE NEW ASSIGNMENT STOP STAY THERE WILL ADVISE STOP.

The signature block showed Marshal Billy Vail's name but Longarm knew better. Billy was more long-winded than that. This message had been composed by Henry on the boss's behalf. Longarm would have bet the ranch on it. Henry was the one who oftimes acted the fussbudget about the office budget.

Not that it mattered. Longarm was ordered to stay here—although what sort of assignment he might be given all the way over here in Nevada he could not figure out—so stay here he would.

He looked down the counter, past the others who were digging into their breakfasts, at the randy, brown-haired gal who ran the place. She surely did not look like the tooth-and-claw wanton that he'd encountered in that back room last night. But then appearances are not nearly as important as performance when it comes to the making of the beast with two backs. And this girl could sure perform in bed.

Before she closed the café and pulled down the blinds, though, there was something Longarm really needed to do.

He was going to have to ask somebody what the hell this gal's name was.

Chuckling softly to himself Longarm put his hat on—carefully, that goose egg was still mighty tender—and went out to stretch his legs and enjoy the morning.

Chapter 8

"Letitia," the barber told him, his hand flying as he whipped the shaving soap into a smooth lather. "The gal as runs the café right over there, right? Letitia Heinrix. But you should know, mister, that it's Missus Heinrix. Her man took off a while back but far as I know they's still married. An' if you could use my advice"—he paused to transfer a dollop of the lather to Longarm's face, smoothing it in place with the side of his thumb— "if you want my advice, I say."

"Glad t' have it if you care to offer it, neighbor," Longarm told him.

The barber grunted and began stropping a razor, the sound of steel on leather rhythmic and soothing. "My advice, since you ask, is for you to forget about that one. Miz Heinrix may be a grass widda, but she takes things serious. She's always been true to that asshole she married."

"Not a good man, eh?"

"Hold still now and don't talk, mister, or I'll slice you wide open."

Longarm grunted but said nothing. The barber began

applying the blade of his razor with a gentle, feathery touch. "No, sir, that little lady deserved better than Ed Heinrix, she surely did. She's a good woman. An' him such a son of a bitch." He tugged Longarm's nose up and held it, stretching the skin so he could get a good cut around the mustache, then picked up some scissors and began trimming the mustache itself and inside Longarm's nose and ears.

"Half the men in town, including more than a few of the married ones, tried to get close to Letitia Heinrix. All the more so when it come clear that Ed wasn't likely coming back. But the lady is true to her vows. She wouldn't give none of them the time of day."

Longarm glanced to see that the barber still had scissors in hand, that his razor had been laid aside for the moment. "Must be hard for her, a woman alone like she is."

The barber shrugged and picked up his razor again, this time smoothing some lather onto the back of Longarm's neck. "Hold still now." Longarm held still. He could hear more than feel the touch of the blade. Funny thing, he reflected. Wherever a man went, the smell of barbershop soap was the same. It was a pleasant scent. Comforting in a way. He liked it.

"She gets along," the barber said. "Or appears to anyhow. She cooks a good meal and gives good value for your money. Most everyone around here eats at Letitia's place one time or another." He took a damp towel out of the coal-fired warming oven and wrapped it around Longarm's face. Damn but that always felt good.

After a few moments—there were two other men in line for the chair, damn it, or Longarm would have wanted to linger under that towel a little longer—he removed the towel and the sheet that covered Longarm's clothes. The man picked up a light whisk and began brushing Longarm's shoulders. "That will be twenty-five cents, sir."

Longarm paid it gladly. Hell, it would have been worth more than that just to avoid the embarrassment of not knowing Letitia Heinrix's name. "Thank you kindly."

He let himself out into the bright sunlight on Grandview's main business street.

He practically felt like he was on vacation, idling around with nothing to do but wait for instructions from the boss.

Resetting his hat at an angle—not trying to be the jaunty tourist but to keep from pressing on that damn goose egg—Longarm ambled away in search of a beverage.

He did not have far to look. Nor any difficulty finding someone to drink with him. When he walked inside the saloon he was greeted by a yelp of welcome.

"Little buddy. Come over here an' join me. An' I won't be taking no for an answer." It was the big bruiser Jacob who had put that goose egg on Longarm's forehead. Today Jacob was grinning like Longarm was a long-lost friend. "Pour one for my pal here," Jacob ordered the barkeep, "and keep them coming. It's on my tab, you hear? His money's no good in here today."

"What the—?"

"I heard what you told Ben Waters. You bailed me outa a lot o' trouble."

"I just made sure he knew the truth, that's all. I was at fault. You shouldn't have to pay for it."

Jacob looked at the bartender and loudly declared, "See why I like this little fella? Now rustle up some drinks for the two of us." He turned to Longarm. "How are you with billiards?"

"I've been known to hold a stick in my hands."

Jacob's grin became even wider. "Come on then. Let's play a little."

There were two young men already playing but they quickly remembered pressing engagements elsewhere when they saw Jacob lumbering toward the table.

How long had it been since he had played a game of billiards, Longarm wondered. Not that it mattered. They were out for pleasure, not for blood. He went to the rack and selected a cue stick that seemed to be reasonably straight, then reached for the chalk and talcum. There were worse ways to pass time in a strange town.

Chapter 9

"All right. You can come out now."

Longarm opened the door and stepped through into the café portion of the building. Letitia had finished locking up for the night and the shades were pulled low over the windows at the front. No one could see in now to discover the prim and proper grass widow's secrets.

He crossed the room and took her into his arms. Letitia pressed her body against his and opened her mouth to his kiss. He felt her tongue probe for his. She tasted of peppermint. After only a moment, though, she pulled away from him and dropped to her knees.

Longarm smiled as Letitia's strong, swift fingers quickly unfastened the buttons at his fly. He started to unbuckle his gun belt, but she pushed his hands aside. "Leave it. I . . . I like it," she whispered.

He nodded. Took his hands away.

Letitia found his cock and pulled it out, already engorged and eager for a warm place to probe.

It found one.

Letitia peeled his foreskin back and rubbed her face over the red bulb that had been hidden there. Her eyelashes fluttered like butterfly wings against his shaft. The tip of her tongue crept out from between her lips and tasted him. Then she opened her mouth wide and pressed her face to him, taking him deep and fast. She gagged but continued pushing forward until the head of his cock invaded her throat.

Longarm braced himself against the counter where each day she served food to her customers. His belt buckle was jammed hard against her forehead and must have hurt, but she seemed not to notice. He could feel her hand on the flat of his ass urging him deeper, deeper.

He closed his eyes and concentrated on the sensations Letitia was creating with those marvelous lips and tongue.

"Got another telegram for you, Marshal."

"Well it's about damn time," Longarm grumbled. This was the fifth day he had spent in Grandview waiting for instructions from the boss. Playing billiards and penny-ante poker during the day. Fucking Letitia at night. It sounded great. A regular vacation but at the government's expense. The truth was that he was becoming bored.

Not a single saloon in the town stocked a first-class rye. He had smoked the last of his good cheroots and was reduced now to a decidedly inferior rum crook. And his prick was sore; Letitia sometimes forgot herself when she was really into the thing and bit down instead of sucking. It was definitely time to be moving along.

Longarm dug into his pocket and found another dime for the delivery boy. He would gladly have given the kid a dollar in exchange for some good news about this new assignment he'd been waiting for.

Then he read the message. It was just as well he had not paid out that dollar or he would have been tempted to go grab the kid and take it back.

INFO KIDNAPPER AKA BLACKBEARD IN GRANDVIEW STOP INFO ON PLAN DEVELOPING STOP INFORMANT EN ROUTE WILL JOIN YOU THERE STOP.

Again the signature block showed Billy's name, but someone else, either Henry or one of the other deputies, must have sent it on his behalf. Billy would have provided more information, even at ten cents a word.

Like, for instance, who the hell this informant was. How was Longarm supposed to know who the son of a bitch was? Or when he would get here?

Not that it really mattered. Whenever he arrived, Longarm would be here waiting for him.

And it would not be difficult for a newcomer to figure out who the visiting deputy U.S. marshal was. Virtually every man, woman, child, and stray dog in Grandview knew him by now.

With any kind of luck, Longarm thought, Billy's informant might arrive on today's stage. If nothing else, that would give him an excuse to avoid sweet Letitia—and those sharp teeth of hers—so his pecker could heal just a little.

In the meantime . . .

"I think it's your turn to break, Jacob."

The big man grinned and thumbed his nose like a prizefighter about to come out for the next round. "You'd best have your best game with you today, little buddy. I feel hot today."

"Naw, that's just the weather you're feelin'. Now pick up that cue stick an' defend yourself. The usual stakes?"

Jacob grunted and bent over the table, already concentrating on how he wanted to play the break.

Chapter 10

Longarm knew something was very seriously wrong the moment he stepped into the café to take his noon meal. Letitia was normally reserved when they were in public, but today she was positively icy. Her face was rigid and her eyes held no more life in them than a bronze statue's.

He wanted to ask what was troubling her but could not. There were customers in the place, including a very attractive young woman he had never seen before. And he thought he had at least seen, if not actually met, all the female residents of Grandview by now.

This gal . . . If it hadn't been for his ongoing involvement with Letitia he would certainly have been tempted to introduce himself. She was young and buxom and dressed well enough for Denver's cosmopolitan soirees. In a place like Grandview she stood out like a boil on a baby's ass.

She had a mass of tight blond curls, a delicately pale complexion, and wide, innocent blue eyes.

Longarm noticed her the moment he stepped inside

41

the café and hung his hat on the rack beside the front door.

It took him scarcely another moment longer, though, to read the rigid set of Letitia's shoulders and the thin, hard line of her lips. Letitia was well and truly pissed off.

Longarm unfastened the bottom button on his vest and straddled his usual stool at the counter. Letitia turned to him and in a prim and businesslike voice asked, "You are the deputy from Denver, aren't you, mister?"

"Mister." Shit, she'd been sleeping with him for the past week and publicly feeding him in this same café and now she was calling him "mister"?

"Yes, ma'am."

Letitia inclined her head toward the pretty blonde. "The lady asked after you."

"What . . . ?" but Letitia had already turned away and was using a spatula to stir a skillet of sliced potatoes. Longarm could hear the pop and sizzle of the grease. He had the impression that Letitia would quite willingly fry him in that lard along with the spuds. Selected parts of him anyway. "Thank you," he said to her back and spun around on the stool.

He stood and crossed the room to the tiny table where the blonde sat nursing a cup of tea. The young woman was seated and Longarm was standing over her, yet she managed to convey the impression that she was looking down her nose at him. And that she did not at all like what she saw when she did. She turned her face away and pretended to ignore him.

"You wanted to see me?"

"I do not customarily speak with stra— Oh!" She clapped a palm over her mouth. "Are you— What is your name, sir?"

"Long, miss. Deputy U.S. Marshal Custis Long."

"Oh, dear. I . . . I assumed . . . something else. I apologize. Yes, I do indeed need to speak with you. Please forgive me, but a woman traveling alone . . . I do hope you understand."

"Of course, miss. Now what can I do for you?"

She looked up, smiling now, and extended a small gloved hand. He dutifully touched her fingertips. "Please, Marshal. Sit down. Would you care for a cup of tea?"

"No, thank you." He glanced toward the counter, hoping to signal Letitia that he would like a cup of coffee, but she was studiously ignoring him. He pulled a chair out and sat opposite the blond girl.

"My name," she began, "is Gloria Ames. And I want you to arrest a man, a kidnapper, who calls himself Blackbeard."

"Blackbeard?"

"Oh, that is not his real name, of course. I do not have that information. I assume this man borrowed the name from the famous pirate Edward Teach."

"I don't know no Teach, Miss Ames. I never seen any fliers out on him."

"The pirate Blackbeard lived a long time ago. But he did kidnap and . . . and ravage." She said the word like it was distasteful to her. "This man continues in that tradition, you might say."

Longarm leaned back and crossed his legs. He reached inside his coat for a smoke.

"Please do not do that, Marshal. I am very sensitive to tobacco smoke."

"Sorry." He put the crook back in his pocket.

"Last year—almost a year ago—this man who calls himself Blackbeard kidnapped my brother. My baby brother. Timothy was only six, a sweet and trusting child. He was at play when he was singled out and taken by this fiend. He was carried off in broad daylight. There were no witnesses. My family . . ." She shuddered and turned her head away.

"My family is . . . was, I should say, well-to-do. My father swore he would get Timmy back. My mother took to her bed with a fever. We waited and a few days later a note was delivered."

"Askin' for ransom?" Longarm asked.

"Exactly. The note demanded that my father place twenty thousand in banknotes into a valise and leave the valise in the manger of an abandoned barn on one of our properties. He did exactly what the note demanded, Marshal. Exactly. He paid the ransom to the very penny. And"—the animation that had begun to illuminate her features dissipated—"we never heard another word. Timmy was never returned to us.

"Losing Timmy like that destroyed my mother's health. She never recovered. She died several months ago, I think of a broken heart more than anything else. My father has been ruined financially. He had to borrow on our properties in order to raise that much cash. Now those are lost as well. And I . . . I have little left, Marshal Long, save the hope that this horrible Blackbeard person can be found and brought to justice for his crimes."

"And you say he's here?"

"That is the information I received, yes. Either he is already here . . . perhaps lives here under his real name . . . or he is coming here. He could be planning new crimes. He could be playing the role of a good citizen. I do not know. What I do know with absolute cer-

44

tainty is that I shall never, sir, *never* abandon my quest to bring this man to justice."

Gloria Ames reached forward and touched Longarm's wrist. "Can you help me, sir? *Will* you help me?"

"I will da . . . uh, dang sure do my level best t' help you, miss," Longarm promised.

Chapter 11

"Join me for lunch, miss? We're gonna need t' talk some more. Might as well accomplish somethin' while we're doin' it," Longarm said.

Gloria frowned. "I do not mean to be ungrateful, but it is not my practice to dine with gentlemen who are not of my class."

"An' what class would that be, miss?" Longarm's voice was syrupy with sarcasm.

Gloria sniffed and frowned at him.

"Never mind, miss. You don't hafta answer. That was what you call a rhetorical question." When she still did not respond he added, "A rhetorical question is—."

"I know what that is, Marshal. Thank you for attempting to instruct me."

"All part of the job, miss."

"Yes. I am sure. I have taken a room, Marshal. I am sharing quarters with Miss Buffington."

Longarm raised an eyebrow in inquiry.

"She is the schoolteacher. She has a home here. The town sheriff suggested I speak with her about living quarters rather than put up in a public house. I took my things in earlier. One advantage to the arrangement is that Miss Buffington is away at the school during the day. That would afford us some privacy if you would care to talk there."

"Sure, that'd be fine."

"Then I shall excuse myself. Enjoy your meal, then join me." She picked up her handbag, and Longarm jumped to his feet so he could help her with her chair. Every other man in the room was watching out of the corners of their eyes. Letitia continued to act like he was leaving a foul odor in the café.

Gloria marched out and this time the menfolk—Custis Long, damn sure included—openly watched her go. Not a bad-looking filly, Longarm concluded. If a bit snotty.

He returned to the lunch counter and sat. After five or six minutes he concluded that he could sit there until his butt grew attached to the stool before Letitia so much as acknowledged he was there.

He got up and went elsewhere in search of his midday meal.

Longarm was bent over a bowl of hog jowl and red beans and was none too happy about it. The beans were burned and the jowl gamey and he was not looking forward to the belly gas the meal was sure to cause. And on top of that, dammit, he just plain did not like the fact that Letitia was mad at him for doing nothing at all.

Well, hardly anything anyway. A guy couldn't help just *looking* at a good-looking woman like Gloria Ames. So his mood was not the best to begin with and then he looked up and saw Ben Waters heading toward him. The town lawman nodded. Longarm returned the favor.

"'Lo, Ben."

Waters pulled out a chair and helped himself to a seat without being invited. He waved to the barkeep and was quickly rewarded with a beer. "Mind if I join you for lunch?" Waters asked.

Longarm felt like snapping back that it appeared he already had. But then that would have been a shitty response to a friendly gesture. Besides, his problem right now was with Letitia, not with Ben.

"Are those beans as bad as they look?" Waters asked.

"Worse."

"Now you know why the little grass widow down the street does a good business."

Longarm took another mouthful and made a sour face. Then dipped up another spoonful of the stuff.

"Did that little woman from Denver find you?"

Longarm nodded. Maybe this shit would go down easier if he didn't chew. Maybe if he just swallowed it he could keep the taste of it off his tongue.

"Said she was looking for somebody name of Black," Waters said. "We don't have any family by that name here, not that I've ever known."

"Blackbeard," Longarm corrected. "Like the old-time pirate."

The marshal seemed confused. "We don't have any pirates neither. Not that I know about."

"She just . . . it's like a nickname. That's what she said anyway."

"I see," Waters said although he quite obviously did not see. He did not have the least inkling what Longarm was talking about.

That was all right, Longarm thought. Hell, he wasn't sure he knew what he was saying either. "She didn't want to talk about it out where she might be overheard. I'm s'posed to meet her this afternoon. D'you know a woman named Buffington?"

"Of course. She's our schoolteacher. A pretty good one too, or so I hear."

"This Miss Ames has taken a room with the teacher."

"Would you like me to show you where the house is?"

Longarm nodded and took another bite of the dreadful beans. He hoped they would not smell as bad later on as they tasted now, but his hopes on that subject were not high.

Chapter 12

The house was small, built of adobe brick with a rickety porch across the front and down one side. A low picket fence that was weathered silver-gray from the sun faced the street. The fence was decorative only—had to be as there was no gate. Inside the fence and along the front of the porch the hard-packed earth had been crumbled and some sort of plants buried. Longarm wasn't sure what they were supposed to be, but now they were bare sticks poking up out of the gravel.

A pair of washtubs and a scrub board were propped against the side wall, and there was a clothesline—empty now—running along the side of the lot.

The house was one of a dozen or so flanking both sides of the block, each identical to the others. Longarm was glad he had Ben with him to act as a guide.

"This is it?"

"Uh-huh," Waters said. "The school is over that direction two blocks away. It should be a couple hours before Miss Buffington gets home."

"All right. Thanks for showing me the way." Longarm entered the yard and stepped up onto the porch. He

51

was mildly surprised to see the town marshal remain at his side. There was no reason for Waters to participate in this meeting.

But then there was no reason why he should not be there either, especially since Grandview was his responsibility and might well be affected by the presence of the kidnapper who called himself Blackbeard.

Waters took the initiative and rapped on the door. A moment later they heard the approach of footsteps and the door was pulled open.

Gloria Ames stood there with a large towel wrapped around her and another arranged turbanlike over her hair. "Excuse me, I . . . I was not expecting you so soon. Please give me a moment, then come in and help yourselves to seats, gentlemen."

She backed away and disappeared, leaving the door cracked partially open.

Waters rolled his eyes. "You reckon she was wearing anything under that towel?"

"I dunno but I'd sure as hell be willin' to look an' see," Longarm responded.

"You and me both."

"I thought you was married."

"I am, but I ain't dead."

They gave Miss Ames time enough to reach the back of the little house, then went in.

The adobe walls and a thick roof made the interior of the place bearable if not actually cool. The furnishings were massive with overstuffed brocade upholstery. Dark curtains fluttered at the open windows, adding to the impression of coolness. It was almost dark enough to require lamps even though it was only the middle of the afternoon.

Longarm and the town marshal settled gingerly onto

a dark green sofa, both of them holding their hats and looking as awkward as the schoolboys whom Miss Buffington taught.

The sounds of movement reached them from behind a closed door that presumably led into a bedroom. Gloria Ames seemed to be taking her time with whatever she was doing in there. A good five minutes passed before she emerged, this time wearing a housedress with a full-length apron covering it. When she walked, Longarm caught a flash of pale color at her ankles that suggested she had not taken the time to put stockings on but had simply stuck her feet into her shoes and quickly buttoned them. Her hair was in disarray, wisps escaping from her bun and falling over her ears. For someone who was supposed to be expecting company she was remarkably ill prepared.

But then perhaps that was her habit, Longarm reflected. Some women seem to go through life disorganized. Gloria Ames could well be one of them.

"Thank you for being patient with me," she said. "May I offer you a refreshment? Lemonade? Or there may be coffee left over from this morning."

"Not for me, thanks."

Ben Waters smiled and nodded. "Lemonade sounds real nice, miss. Thank you."

Longarm gave the man a slightly exasperated look. This was not the town marshal's interview and Longarm had not especially wanted him here. Now it was obvious that not only was he here but he also fully expected to remain for the duration.

Miss Ames said, "I will only be a moment," then disappeared again, this time through a different doorway that obviously led into the kitchen.

Waters nudged Longarm with his elbow and whispered, "I liked her other outfit better'n this one."

53

Longarm said nothing. He liked that first outfit better too and had to think that if Ben hadn't tagged along with him he might just have been able to find out what was underneath that towel. There was no chance of that now though.

Darn it.

Chapter 13

"Y'know, miss," Longarm said, "for someone who's come all the way here from Kansas to tell us something, you ain't exactly sayin' very much."

Gloria Ames looked down her nose at him and at Ben Waters. "I do not know what you intend by that remark."

"I mean you're the one as s'posed to know something about this Blackbeard fella, so what is it that brought you all this way?"

"I already told you that—."

"What you said was that you got information. Fine. The law needs information. Deals with it all the time. So just what exactly is this information?"

"I told you. This Blackbeard person is said to already be here in Grandview or soon shall be."

"Right. Whoever he is. Which you don't know an' can't tell us. Why, miss, you ain't even told us how you come by this knowledge."

"I also told you that—."

"Yeah, yeah." Longarm waved his hand dismissively. "You can't say anything 'bout that without violating a confidence. Well, miss, you ain't giving us anything t' go on. You don't know the fella's true name or what names he might be using around here. You don't know what he looks like. Don't know how old he is. You just ain't giving us anything t' go on, miss. I hate to say that, but it's so."

Waters leaned forward and said, "I know pretty much everyone around here, Miss Ames. If you can just think of a little more for us to work with. Anything at all . . ."

Gloria Ames dragged a handkerchief out of her sleeve and began to sob into it, her shoulders shaking and her lips quivering. "I told you everything I know," she wailed. "What do you want from me? Why are you treating me like I am the criminal? Why must you be like this? What about my baby brother? What about my mama's broken heart? Stop it. Please stop this. I cannot stand it. I really cannot."

Her eyes were moist and puffy and her complexion was mottled with patches of red, and a stream of snot ran from her nose to her lip and into the corner of her pouting mouth.

Some women are sexy when they cry. They make a man want to soothe and comfort them. And some simply make a man want to drop their knickers and fuck them.

Gloria Ames looked like shit when she bawled. Bedraggled and unattractive. He couldn't speak for Ben Waters, but Longarm's reaction was a sudden desire to be somewhere else until the girl got hold of herself and quit leaking all over herself.

He and Waters rode out the storm. It took a good while. Then Longarm stood. "Thank you for your help, miss. The marshal an' me will talk this over. See if we can come up with any ways how this, uh, information o' yours can be of any use."

56

The girl looked up, her eyes moving from Longarm to Waters and back again. "Is that all?" She sounded surprised.

"D'you got anything more you can tell us, miss?"

"No. I already told you everything I know."

"Except how you come by the knowledge," Longarm said with a frown.

"But I've explained that. I . . . I cannot say anything about that."

"Yeah, well, me an' the marshal will talk this over."

"If there is anything else I can do," the girl offered, "all you need do is ask. Come by anytime. I mean that, Marshal Long. Anytime."

The men said their good-byes and left, heading back into the late-afternoon heat as soon as they stepped off the schoolteacher's front porch.

"That was a waste o' good time," Longarm grumbled once they reached the street. "I coulda been accomplishing something important instead. Like drinkin' beer an' playing billiards."

Waters cleared his throat. "I'm sure it has already occurred to you that perhaps the young lady is reluctant to say anything with me there. After all, she claims this kidnapper could live here. If all the male residents of Grandview are suspects then I don't suppose there is any reason to eliminate me from them. She said she doesn't know who the man is. She could suspect me along with all the others in town."

Longarm did not particularly want to say so, but the truth was that it was a possibility he had thought of too. "D'you mean you wouldn't be offended if I was t' talk with the lady again in private?"

"Certainly not. If what she says is true, then the sooner we find him the better."

Longarm nodded. "Good. Then if you don't mind . . ."

He turned back the way they had just come and headed back toward the Buffington house. "If I learn anything more, Ben, I'll let you know."

Once again Longarm turned in at the gap where a gate should have been and mounted the porch at the front of the schoolteacher's place.

Chapter 14

"Yes? Oh, it's you, Marshal." She stepped back from the door. "Please come in."

He did, hat in hand, and returned to the same place on the sofa where he had sat a few minutes earlier.

"What may I do for you, Marshal?"

Longarm took a moment to look her over. In the brief period since he and Ben Waters had left the house, Gloria had managed to refresh her appearance. There was no longer so much as a hint of the red-faced, blubbering mess she had been when she was crying. Her eyes were dry and clear. Her hair was tucked tidily in place. He was not sure but thought she might even have applied a pale blush of rouge to enhance the color of her lips and her cheeks. Gloria was once again the enormously attractive young woman. All of that in the time it had taken him to walk a block down the street and back again. He was impressed.

There was something else that seemed different about her too, although damned if he could get a handle on just exactly what that "something" was.

Something about . . . the way she was looking at him

perhaps? He got the impression that the girl was weighing her thoughts. Judging. He opened his mouth to speak, intending to ask if anything had changed, thought better of it, and closed his mouth again.

"Yes? You were going to say something?"

"Yeah, I, uh, I wondered was there anything you wanted t' say that you wouldn't feel comfortable talkin' about in front o' Grandview's town marshal."

"Oh, dear. Do you mean to ask if I could suspect him of being the kidnapper?"

Longarm nodded. "Him bein' local an' all."

"That possibility had not actually occurred to me. How very stupid of me not to think of that."

"It ain't the sort o' thing a young an' pretty girl should have to be thinkin' about, miss. An' there's no harm done. If there is anything you can tell me now an' no harm done."

Gloria dropped her face into her hands and . . . he was not entirely sure but thought she giggled just a little bit.

Or she could have been sobbing.

"Is there something wrong, miss?"

She looked up again. And no, she was not crying. "Did you say 'young and pretty,' Marshal? Do you mean that?"

"I always mean what I say." And if that was a lie, it was a small white one at the worst. Besides, no female ever hates a compliment regardless of what they might say or do in response to one.

"Do you mind if I ask you a personal question, Marshal?"

"Go ahead."

"How tall are you?"

Longarm blinked. There was a mighty long list of other things Longarm might have expected the girl to ask before she would have gotten around to that one. As

60

it was, her curiosity threw him a little off stride. Again he opened his mouth to speak, thought better of it, and clamped his lips closed. He settled for a shrug.

His response set Gloria to giggling again. She hid her face in her hands and this time he was pretty sure she was chuckling.

"We, uh, maybe we oughta get back t' the reason I'm here, miss," he suggested.

Gloria sat upright and arranged her features into a solemn and quite serious look. "Yes. Of course. I'm sorry." She did not sound particularly sorry. If anything he thought she looked quite impish. But she did say it, and she did keep a straight face when she did so. "Go ahead. Please."

"Yes, miss. Now about this kidnapper an' how you come t' hear whatever you heard—."

Gloria came swiftly to her feet, forcing Longarm to grab his Stetson off his lap and also stand.

"Will you excuse me for a moment, Marshal?"

He blinked. "I, uh . . . o' course."

"I won't be a minute."

"Take your time."

"Which reminds me, do you happen to know the time?"

"Now? What time it is right now?"

She nodded.

Longarm transferred his hat to his other hand and pulled the bulbous Ingersoll from his vest pocket. "Two forty-seven," he said.

Gloria nodded. "School lets out promptly at three thirty. Miss Buffington will be home a few minutes after that."

"So we got better'n a half hour t' talk before she gets here," Longarm said.

Gloria smiled. "Exactly." She seemed pleased.

The girl spun away with a swirl of cloth and the rustle of starched crinolines. "I will not be long."

Longarm was not sure but he thought . . . dammit, the truth was that he thought Gloria Ames was feeling a mite amorous. Certainly she was acting the coquette all of a sudden.

He could see it in the way she held herself. Her body posture and her facial expressions . . . and in where her eyes kept drifting when she was looking at him. He would almost have sworn that she was stealing peeks at his fly.

As soon as Gloria had disappeared into a back room, he quickly reached down and checked to make sure he was all buttoned up, with nothing hanging out for the world to see. It was all right though. No buttons had fallen off or come undone.

He resumed his seat on the sofa and when he did so became aware of a growing pressure at his backside.

Those beans! Oh, shit. Those lousy beans were beginning to rumble and groan in his gut.

Giving a quick glance in the direction of the bedroom where Gloria had gone, he tilted his butt up on one cheek and let a little of the pressure out.

That felt good but, damn, it stank.

His fart smelled like what a buzzard would puke up if it ate a long-dead skunk.

Stench like that would drop a housefly at twenty paces.

And there was more where that came from.

He scarcely had time to enjoy the relief of that first one before he could feel another building.

Why in *hell* had he had those miserable damned beans!

He could hear Gloria moving around on the other side of that door. Changing clothes again? Or simply removing some?

He really did have the impression that she was interested in doing a bit of the nasty, never mind that innocent young girls did not do that sort of thing with perfect strangers.

But . . . he tipped over to the side and let more gas escape. This one smelled even worse than the first had. If this continued, dammit, he was going to have to borrow a safety valve from the Denver and Rio Grande and shove it up his own ass just to keep his guts from swelling up and exploding.

Gloria Ames was a pretty girl. But he did not know, not for sure, what she was doing behind that closed door. And he for damn sure did not want to asphyxiate her with these evil gases. Regardless of whatever her intentions might—or might not—be.

Longarm could hear the *clink* of glass on glass. The stopper on a perfume bottle perhaps? It sounded like that.

Once again the pressure in his gut threatened to overwhelm him, and this time there was a brief growl of muted thunder to accompany the stink.

Very, very quietly Longarm stood up and slipped outside to the safety of the front porch and open air.

He did not so much as look back as he quickstepped toward the nearest alley where he might find an outhouse.

Chapter 15

Longarm waited in the shadows across the street until he saw Letitia pull the shades down over the café windows, then he slipped around into the alley and tapped lightly on the back door.

"Custis! Where have you been? I missed you at supper."

He blinked, taken completely aback by her smile and friendly tone of voice. "Missed me? Why, I thought you'd decided that you hate my guts an' never wanted me t' darken your door again."

She frowned. "Whatever gave you . . . Oh!" She laughed softly. "I'm sorry. Really. I just, well, that girl is so pretty. And I suppose that I thought . . . I know you stopped by to see her this afternoon, and I know that Marshal Waters was with you at the time. So it does not really matter what I thought."

"You don't want me t' pick up my things an' clear out then?"

"Certainly not." Letitia quickly glanced in both directions down the alley, then reached out and pulled Longarm inside the café. Without even bothering to first close the door, she wrapped herself tightly around him, ground her belly against his and tried to lick his tonsils. "Does that tell you anything?" she challenged, her breathing harsh now and rapid.

"Hmm, I'd say it raises some possibilities," he drawled.

Letitia laughed and said, "That is not all it raised." She made her meaning clear by reaching between their bodies and taking hold of the bulge in his britches.

Longarm stepped across the threshold and shoved the door shut behind him, then took the woman into his arms and did a thorough job of taking the rest of her breath away.

Letitia placed her cheek against his chest and closed her eyes. After a moment she lifted her face and delicately whispered, "Fuck me."

"Happy t' be of service, ma'am. Happy t' be of service."

"Ouch!"

"Sorry."

"Watch that elbow."

"I said I was sorry." He grinned. "If I was t' spend very much time here I think I'd hafta buy you a bigger bed. This little bunk makes things difficult."

She very lightly nipped his earlobe. Her breath was warm and her voice soft. "I like being so close to you."

"Close is good," he agreed. "But it can be taken too far."

"Do you want me to sleep on the floor?"

Longarm paused, then said, "Y'know, if we was t' pull these blankets down and lay 'em out we'd have us a sort of pallet. Hard but plenty o' room to . . . whatever."

"I like 'whatever.' "

66

"Yeah, I kinda noticed that."

"More room to thrash around."

"Uh-huh."

Letitia jumped up, launching herself off the bed in a single bound. "Get up," she instructed. "I can't get those things off the bed while you're lying on top of them."

He took his time about sitting up and when he did he said, "Turn up the lamp a little, please."

"Oh, I don't need any more light just to lay out a pallet."

Longarm smiled. "It ain't for you that I want the light, woman. It's so I can see to admire that fine body o' yours." He reached for a cigar. "Has anybody ever told you that you got marvelous legs?"

"No."

"Well, you do."

"What is so special about them?"

He chuckled. "They reach all the way up to that pretty ass, that's what. Now quit fishing for compliments an' get us a pallet laid down 'cause I ain't wore out quite yet. I'm wanting some more o' that sweet pussy."

"Then get the hell out of my way, mister, before you get hurt. And from now on, I would advise you to never, but never, stand between me and a good fuck."

Longarm got the hell out of her way.

Chapter 16

Longarm was only dimly aware of the movement when Letitia left the pallet and the warm nest they had created there. He felt a spill of chill air on his bare skin when she swept the blanket aside, but a moment later she laid it over him again and even tucked it in under his chin. A flicker of smile tugged at his lips. Then he drifted back into the slumber of exhaustion. The girl had purely worn him out—not that he was complaining.

When he woke again, it was broad daylight outside and he could hear the voices of the breakfast crowd out in the public area of the café. The buzz of conversations and the clatter of pots and dishware had a comforting, homey sound. Longarm smiled, satisfied, and took a moment to enjoy the slow, languid process of wakening to a new day.

Lying abed, awake but not yet busy with the problems of the day that was yet to come, was a good time to think. And one of the things that crossed Longarm's mind on this morning was that he was one lucky son of a bitch. He had work that he was good at and at the same time actually enjoyed. He had staunch friends.

Good health. A man could not ask for much more than that, could he?

After a few moments of introspection he swept the blanket aside and stood, shivering just a little in the cool of the morning as he quickly dressed and belted the big Colt at his waist. As always, he took a few extra seconds to make sure the butt of the revolver lay in exactly the right spot for speed and comfort. Then he tugged his brown Stetson firmly on his head and slipped out the back door.

He walked through the alley, weaving his way around mounds of trash, and helped himself to the use of one of the outhouses that lined the public alley, then continued on to the next street and ambled around to the front of the building that included Letitia's café.

On the boardwalk he encountered Marshal Ben Waters. "Mornin', Ben. Where are you off to at this time of day?"

"Good morning, Longarm." The marshal patted his belly. "I just finished breakfast. Going back to my office now. You?"

"On my way to the café over here to get a bite. You're welcome to join me. We need to talk about this Blackbeard thing."

"I reckon I could stand one more cup of coffee." Waters did an about-face and headed back the way he had just come.

The café was busy but not overcrowded. Longarm and the marshal found a table toward the back of the place. It was separated by only a few rough-hewn boards from the pallet where Longarm had wakened minutes earlier.

Letitia set two plates down in front of some men at the counter, then came over to take Longarm's and Ben

70

Waters's orders. Without being asked, she brought two steaming cups of coffee with her, setting one before each man. "Good morning, gentlemen. What would you like?"

Longarm almost burst out laughing. Letitia sounded so detached and businesslike. Very professional. He could not help but think about how pretty she was when she had his cock in her mouth. Or how it felt when he speared her deep inside that tidy little ass. Oh, she did thrash and shudder and squeal when she was in the throes of passion. Now there was not the faintest hint of that, however.

"You've already taken care of me," Waters said. "This coffee will do me fine, Miz Heinrix, thank you."

"And for you, sir?" she asked, looking down at Longarm.

"A plate o' whatever you got. Taters and some fried pig meat or whatever you got on hand over there."

"Yes, sir." She turned and went back to her stoves, her tight and tidy butt swaying from side to side and both men watching the movement.

"Nice," Waters mumbled before he turned his attention back to Longarm.

"I agree," Longarm said.

"About this Blackbeard thing . . ." Waters said.

Longarm took a sip of his coffee. It was hot and strong and cleansed his mouth after the many uses he had put it to during the night. "Have you been thinkin' about it, Ben?"

The town marshal nodded. "We don't know if Blackbeard is someone who lives here or a stranger coming in to cause mischief. The way I see it, if he does live here he won't be pulling off any kidnappings here."

Longarm nodded. "I agree. He'd want to keep any pursuit or suspicion away from his home place."

"Right. So there wouldn't be any clues to trip him up. Nothing to call attention to himself, at least not as a kidnapper."

"Which makes him mighty damn hard to locate," Longarm said, "even with your help. Which, by the way, I do appreciate."

Letitia arrived carrying a huge platter of pork chops and fried spuds. She set it in front of Longarm, checked to make sure the level of coffee in their cups was not yet low, and returned to her work, washing dishes between waiting tables and cooking.

"That is a handsome woman," Waters mused. He looked at Longarm's platter and said, "I think she likes you. She's never served me that many chops."

"You want one? There's enough here to share."

"No, I'm full, thanks. But getting back to Blackbeard, I've been nosing around, looking to see what we have for strangers right now."

"Find any likely prospects that might be him?"

Waters nodded. "I think I did. One of the kids I talked to—young boys are a fine source of information sometimes, you know—told me he saw a stranger camped out at Parkers Spring. That is a seep of potable water out southeast of town. Antelope and small critters water there although there isn't enough for livestock. It's a slow seep into a small basin. Most folks don't even know it's there."

"But this stranger does," Longarm mused.

"So it seems."

"I think after breakfast, Ben, we should ride out there. If you'd be kind enough t' show me the way, that is."

Waters nodded, and Longarm dug into his meal, in something of a hurry now to finish eating and go see if this stranger at the hidden water hole could indeed be the kidnapper who called himself Blackbeard.

Chapter 17

There were only two saddle horses available at Dud James's Grandview livery: bad and worse. God knew what the worse animal would have been like; the bad one was bad enough.

It had a hard mouth and a mean disposition. The first thing it did when Longarm stepped next to it was crane its head around and try to take a bite out of his ass. He chopped it on the nose with the edge of his hand hard enough to hurt him, never mind the son-of-a-bitch brown horse.

The beast laid its ears back and tried to strike with its left fore. Longarm stepped closer, dropped his shoulder, and shoved. The horse fell heavily onto its side, then scrambled onto its feet again.

"Good boy," Longarm crooned gently. "That's the boy."

The brown tossed its head, pinned its ears again and tried to nip his shoulder. This time Longarm socked it as hard as he could just behind the jaw. The horse rolled its eyes but did not offer to bite again. It stood reasonably still while Longarm took his time about getting his saddle securely placed and his bit and bridle properly adjusted.

"Fine animal you have here," he mumbled to the hostler as he led the brown out of the barn.

"Hell, mister, you ain't seen nothing yet."

"That good, is he?"

"Uh-huh. Only reason he ain't dead is that I got no dogs to feed him to. That and the fac' that he's a sight better than the other one."

"Hard to believe any one man could own *two* horses this bad."

"Just lucky, I guess." Dud James cackled, showing pink gums where teeth ought to be.

Longarm swung onto his saddle and immediately braced himself for a storm, but all the brown did was reach around and try to bite his kneecap.

"He's not a bucker," the hostler said, "just meaner than a son of a bitch."

"How bad is the other one?" Longarm asked, reaching for a cigar and lighting it.

"That one has to buck a good five minutes every time somebody climbs onto him. And I do mean *every* time, even if you've just stepped down to open a gate. That one"—he pointed his chin toward the brown Longarm was sitting—"he'll kick your brains out if you give him the chance, but he's got a decent way of going, and I don't know as it would be possible to wear him out. He's tough. Just you be tougher."

"Him and me will get along all right," Longarm said. He let a stream of rum-scented smoke out of his nostrils, then touched the brim of his hat to the hostler before reining away.

He met Ben Waters at the edge of town. The marshal was mounted on a little speckled mare that was pretty

74

enough to be a pet. And probably was. The mare's mane was braided and its hoofs painted the boot black.

"D'you got a daughter?" Longarm asked.

Waters laughed. "How did you guess? Yes, this is Esther's pony. She lets me borrow it if I ask nice."

Longarm nodded. "Lead the way, Ben. Let's go see if we got us a landlocked pirate in the neighborhood."

Chapter 18

Ben Waters drew rein about an hour out of town—well outside his legal jurisdiction—and motioned for Longarm to move up beside him. Longarm's brown tried to take a bite out of Waters's mare, and Longarm kicked him in the jaw, which settled him down at least for the moment.

"The other side of this rise," Waters said, gesturing toward a low hogback in front of them, "is a sort of swale with some rock and creosote in it. Parkers Spring is at the base of a cluster of boulders. The seep is located in among the rocks. We won't know where this Blackbeard is—if it's Blackbeard, that is—until we look down in there, but if I was doing it I'd lay out on top of the biggest of those rocks so's I could see all around without no obstructions."

"Makes sense," Longarm agreed. He pulled a rum crook out of his pocket and stuck it in the corner of his jaw but did not light it. He did not want the sight or possibly the scent of cigar smoke to give them away before they were ready to announce themselves to whomever it was who was camping down there.

"You have more experience with this sort of thing," Waters said, "so you're welcome to take charge now that we've got here."

"It's more a matter o' the two of us workin' together than either one of us bein' in charge, but what I'd suggest is that we leave the horses here an' belly up to the top of this rise. Take a look to the other side an' see what we're up against before we lay any plans."

He took the cigar out of his mouth and wistfully inspected the cold, virgin tip but resisted the temptation to light up. Then he said, "Reckon it's best to make the plan fit the situation 'stead of the other way around. So let's go have us a look-see. Then we'll talk."

Waters nodded and stepped down from his mare. Longarm reined the brown a couple rods away before he dismounted. He did not want to trust a strange animal to ground tie so took the time to hobble the rented horse and also secured the reins to a man-tall creosote. No way did he want to walk back to Grandview in this heat.

"Ready?"

"Uh-huh."

Longarm carried his Winchester in a relaxed imitation of the army's port arms position, held in both hands and slanted across his body, ready for a snap shot if necessary. Waters was armed only with his pip-squeak little nickel-plated revolver.

There was a gradual slope leading to the top of the hogback, and they had to walk a hundred yards or so before they dropped to a crouch and finally to a crawl to gain the summit.

"There," Waters whispered when they were in position.

Longarm grunted. "I wish I'd thought to bring my field glasses along."

"Are they in your saddlebags? I could run back and get them for you," the Grandview marshal offered.

"Thanks, but they're in my room back in Denver."

"Then you would have to give me a note for your landlord," Waters said, sounding so deadpan serious that Longarm had to look at him to see the twinkle in his eyes to realize the marshal was pulling his leg. Ben Waters was growing on him.

Longarm returned his attention to the matter at hand, tugging his hat brim a little lower and shading his eyes with his hands cupped on both sides of his face to cut the midday glare.

"Do you see anything?" Waters asked.

"No, I . . . Wait a minute. On top of that rock."

"The big one?"

"No, just to the left of it and a little bit lower. There. I thought I saw something move."

"It could be a chuckwalla lizard."

"Yeah, or it could be a man's head. I think . . . there. Did you see it this time?"

"Uh-huh. Looks like a hat, don't it?"

"That's what I'm thinking," Longarm agreed. "Now, why would a man lie out in the middle of a hot day like that except t' keep watch for his enemies?"

"And what enemies might those be, eh?"

Longarm chewed on the now soggy end of his cigar for a moment before he answered. "That could be an innocent prospector down there who doesn't want to risk having a claim jumped. Could be some fella who's got some gal in the family way an' is scared of her pap or her brothers. Could be a thousan' perfectly lawful reasons why a fella might want to have hisself some privacy out here. Hell, he could be a pilgrim down there

79

fasting an' praying or something. We can't go in shooting an' raising hell with him. Not without knowing a little more."

"What do you propose then, Longarm?"

For several minutes Longarm lay there chewing on
the rum crook and examining the all too open terrain
that lay between them and the nest of rocks where the
unknown party was holed up. Finally he grunted and began slithering back off the ridgeline out of sight.

"All right," he said when they were far enough below
the crest that they could sit up again. "I got a plan if
you're willin' to go along with it."

Chapter 19

Longarm checked his Ingersoll, then tucked the watch back into his vest pocket. Twenty minutes he had said and twenty minutes it was. The midday heat burned across his shoulders even through the tweed of his coat, and down beyond the nest of rocks where the unknown camper waited, the sagebrush and caliche shimmered in the glare of the sun. It had taken Longarm ten minutes to get into position. The other ten he had spent thinking about all the things that could go wrong with his plan.

It was his idea, though, so he likely would get no sympathy from Ben Waters if he started complaining about it now. Longarm stood and shaded his eyes. It was a good mile and a quarter down to the spot he was watching but after a moment he could see a dark figure, made tall and elongated by heat distortion, coming into view and very slowly walking a horse toward the hidden seep.

Longarm gave the watcher time to spot Ben headed toward him and then, while his attention should be on Waters, Longarm slipped out of hiding and began sneaking up on the rocks from the opposite direction. He stayed in a low crouch as best he could to take advantage of the scattered brush that dotted the flat. It would have been safer to scramble along on hands and knees but that would have been slow. If he tried to do that for his own safety, Ben would be within rifle range long before Longarm could come up behind the gunman.

He tossed the thoroughly chewed but never lit cigar onto the ground and concentrated on getting close to those rocks before any shooting started. When—if—it did, Longarm intended to be the one doing most of it.

From this angle he could see the hidden gunman's horse. It was a scrawny bay with a roached mane. Its owner might not know Longarm was in the vicinity but the horse certainly did. Its ears were swiveled in his direction, and it shifted around impatiently to present its butt, ready to kick if he should try to come up on it from behind.

Up on top of the rocks, the man—he had a rifle close to hand, Longarm could see as he came near—was concentrating on Ben Waters coming up from the south. At the moment though he held a spyglass while the rifle lay at his side.

While Longarm watched, the fellow carefully collapsed the spyglass into itself, slid it into a fitted leather case, and buckled the case closed.

Then he picked up his rifle.

Longarm froze in place. He was still farther away than he would like to be. Close enough to shoot if he had to, but far enough away that he would rather not. He was beginning to regret his decision to leave his Winchester in its scabbard hanging on that fool son-of-a-bitch horse. He'd intended to get in close enough for pistol work, which was faster. But if that were not possible, the tough luck could be Ben's. Longarm stretched his legs even though he was concerned now about the rifleman hearing his footsteps.

Another few strides, just a few, and he would be close enough to be sure of his shot if he had to shoot in a hurry. He was already close enough for an aimed shot . . . if he had time to aim and carefully squeeze.

Or, more accurately, if *Ben* had time for him to aim and squeeze. As long as the guy with the rifle did not know he was there, Longarm had all the time in the world, Ben Waters being the one riding out in front of that rifle muzzle.

Longarm slowed, placing his feet with care now, trying to be as quiet as possible.

The rifleman crouched on top of his perch, then took a deep breath. He stood, holding the rifle across his belly. He lifted one hand and cupped it beside his mouth.

"Is that you, Ben?" His voice boomed across the sun-baked earth.

Down to the south Waters drew rein. "Harry?" His voice was thin at that distance.

"It's me, Ben. What're you doin' here?"

"I heard there was somebody hiding out here, Harry. I didn't know it was you though."

"Turn your horse and ride wide of me, Ben. Go back to town. You ain't the law out here. Your badge don't take you no farther than the town limits."

"I can't do that, Harry." Waters slowed his mare to a walk but came on.

"Nobody knows about this, Ben. Nobody but you an' me, and I damn sure won't tell if'n you don't."

"You're wrong, Harry. There's a deputy U.S. marshal that knows."

"He'll only know if you tell him, Ben. You don't have

to say nothing." The man called Harry lifted his carbine higher and dragged the hammer back to full cock. By then Longarm was close enough to clearly hear the *click* of the sear engaging. "Turn away, Ben. Don't make me shoot you."

"Put it down, Harry. Put the gun down."

"I'm warning you, Ben."

Longarm opened his mouth to deliver a warning of his own, but he had left it too late.

Harry's rifle snapped up to his shoulder and he leaned over the sights. Waters was not more than thirty yards distant and was a sitting duck to a man with a rifle.

Longarm's hand flashed, and his Colt swept out and up, the muzzle seeking the man standing on top of the rocks.

Longarm fired first. His slug tore into the thick pad of muscle beneath the shoulder blade of the rifleman. Harry's finger clenched involuntarily, and his Winchester spat flame. A moment later the rifle dropped out of Harry's suddenly nerveless fingers to clatter onto the boulder and slide down onto the gravel beside the little life-giving seep of fresh water.

"Well, shit!" Longarm grumbled aloud.

Chapter 20

"His name is Harry Bannister," Waters said, kneeling beside the wounded man. "There's paper out on him."

"I didn' . . . didn' . . . do it, Ben. Am I dying?" Bannister was a young fellow, just barely on either side of twenty, Longarm guessed. A good-looking kid, too, with dark, curly hair and the seedy beginnings of a beard.

"We don't know, Harry. We'll fix you up."

"Bullshit," Longarm said. "You're dying, man. Whatever you done, you need to get it off your conscience before you go under. Tell us while you still can or go t' your maker carryin' that load on you."

Ben looked up and gave Longarm a sharp look, obviously not disagreeing that the man was dying but whether he should be told about it.

"I didn't do . . . what they said," Bannister mumbled, bloody froth appearing on his lips. Longarm's bullet had passed through his lung and emerged from his chest, tearing a gaping hole in the plate of bone and cartilage there. Dark blood was spreading over his chest and pooling at his waist before spilling onto the hard ground where he lay.

"The girl swears that you did, Harry."

"She . . . wanted it . . . Ben. Said . . . yes. Her daddy caught . . . us. That's when she hollered . . . rape. I didn' do that, Ben. I wouldn'. Katie puts out for . . . for all the guys. Why would I rape her?"

"I'm not interested in that," Longarm injected. "What about the kidnapping?"

Bannister frowned. "Kid . . . nap? We was in . . . in the church. I didn' take her no place. Not . . ." A spate of coughing wracked his body, and he twisted in pain. Waters pulled the boy's bandana off and dipped it into the seep, then used it to mop his forehead and wipe some of the blood away from his mouth. There was no point in trying to clean up the blood that was still flowing out of the hole in his chest.

Waters looked up at Longarm, who was standing over the two of them. "Our preacher, Charlie Jones, is the one who swore out the warrant. His daughter Katie said he raped her. Right there in the sanctuary."

"Look, Bannister, I don't give a shit if you raped half the women in this county and talked dirty to the rest of 'em. What I want to know is about those folks you kidnapped. I want to know about Timothy Ames. You remember him. Little guy. Six years old. You took the ransom money but nobody ever saw the boy again. You killed him and ruined his whole family. That's the kidnap I want to know about."

Bannister looked at Ben Waters. "What's he saying, Ben? That I did some . . . something . . ." He coughed and more red froth bubbled on his lips. "Something to some little kid? I never, Ben. I swear it. I never hurt no kid. Never hurt Katie neither. She . . . she likes it, Ben. Ask anybody."

Waters bathed Bannister's forehead with the damp bandana and took a firm grip on his hand. "I know you didn't, Harry. I know."

"But Katie . . ."

"I believe you, Harry. It's all right."

"You promise, Ben? You believe me? You really do?"

"Yeah, kid. I really do." He had been kneeling beside Bannister. Now he sat down, still holding Harry's hand. Longarm gathered that the town marshal was prepared to sit there giving whatever comfort he could for as long as it took. Until Harry Bannister died.

Ben looked up at Longarm again. "If I'd known it was Harry out here I could have told you that he didn't do any kidnapping back in Colorado or Nebraska or wherever it was. Harry rides for the J Z Bar outfit, the Jazzy. He hasn't missed a Saturday night fandango since the boys got back from the last cattle drive up to the rails."

"Sorry," Longarm said. "I wish I'd known too. But he was fixing to shoot. I couldn't let him do that."

"Just gonna warn him, mister. I wouldn' of shot Ben. I wouldn' never."

"I believe you, Harry," Waters said solicitously. He looked up. "Longarm, would you wet this for me again, please? I can't reach the water sitting down like this."

"Sure." He dipped the cloth into the seep, wrung a little of the surplus moisture out, and handed the bandana back to the marshal.

"Kid," Longarm said, "I'm sorry as all hell that I've gone an' killed you. I thought you was gonna shoot Ben. I hope you understand that."

"Yes, sir." Harry nodded. "I do, sir. But I sure as hell wisht you hadn' gone and killed me." He began to cry. "I didn' do what Preacher Jones said. Honest I didn'."

Longarm sighed. "Take care of the boy, Ben. I'll fetch my horse and take care of them. Take them some water an' like that. You just take care of the boy."

They had not come prepared for a long siege and had no food with them, but Longarm thought he had a little coffee in his saddlebags. He had no coffeepot with him but he did have a quart-size tin cup that he used for a hundred different purposes. He could boil some coffee in that and share the cup with Ben Waters.

The best he could hope for now though was that the kid would go ahead and die soon. Not that Longarm wished him ill. To the contrary, he was hoping that the youngster's pain would soon be ended.

"Shit," he mumbled as he turned to start the hike back to where he had left the hard-mouthed and evil-tempered livery horse.

Chapter 21

When Longarm woke to a new dawn, Ben Waters was still sitting beside young Harry Bannister, but now the boy's hands were crossed on his belly and his eyes had been covered with pennies.

"When'd he go?" Longarm asked.

"Couple hours ago. Something like that. I didn't see no reason to wake you."

"D'you want me to make another cup of coffee?"

"Thanks but I'd rather get on back to town now. I need to see to the burying and notify the foreman out at the Jazzy. Maybe they know how to reach Harry's folks, wherever they are."

"Want me to write the letter to them? After all, I'm the one as killed their boy."

Waters shook his head. "That won't be necessary, Longarm. I'll take care of it."

"Whatever you think."

Longarm walked away from the rocks and hazed the horses in. He had hobbled them and turned them loose to find whatever graze they could. Now he used his hat to carry water to each of them, emptying the seep in the process.

"It's a good thing we aren't trying to make coffee now," Waters said.

"Yeah, ain't it."

The town marshal continued to sit beside the dead boy, so Longarm saddled all three horses, then helped Ben load Bannister belly-down over his mount. They looped his belt over the saddle horn and ran a piggin string under the horse's belly securing his hands and feet in place. The body would flop around some but probably not fall off.

"Ready?"

"Yeah. Dammit."

Waters took the reins to lead Bannister's horse, and Longarm mounted the hammerhead. He only had to whack the horse in the nose twice to get it to stand without biting.

The ride back to Grandview was completed in silence except for the soughing of a west wind and the clop of the horses' hoofs on hard earth.

They reached town before noon. "I'll take the boy over to Jimmy Sligh. He does whatever laying out needs to be done around here," Waters said.

"Me, I'm heading for the café. I want that coffee we didn't take time for this morning." Longarm smiled. "And enough grub for breakfast *and* the supper we didn't get around to last night. Join me if you like. I'll buy."

"Thanks but I think not. I have a lot to do." Waters's expression hardened. "Including talking with Charlie Jones. Him and that loose daughter of his are the ones who caused Harry's death. I intend to make sure the preacherman understands that."

"Good luck with it, but if I had to lay money it would be on the side of him denying his little angel could do such a thing."

"Harry was right, you know. That girl will spread her knees for any boy that wants her. Spread her knees or drop onto them, whichever the boy wants. Or so I hear tell. That isn't a voice of experience, understand."

"It never crossed my mind," Longarm said. "But tell me something, Ben. Back there when you seen who our fugitive was . . . if I hadn't been along with you, you would've turned around an' headed back to town, wouldn't you?"

Ben nodded. "I would have, Longarm. Oh, I would've told myself that I didn't have jurisdiction outside the town limits. And that would have been the truth. But yeah, knowing the Jones girl and her straitlaced papa, I would've turned back even if I did have the lawful authority to continue."

"I'm sorry, Ben. I am truly sorry."

Waters shrugged. "There's no help for it now."

Longarm dismounted and took a quick step to the side to avoid having a chunk taken out of his upper arm by the horse. "Quit, you ugly son of a bitch." He smacked the horse in the jaw and felt like he damn near broke his hand on the shelf of hard bone there.

"The worst part," he said, looking up at Waters, who was still in the saddle, "is that we're right back where we started when it comes to finding this Blackbeard. He could be 'most anybody. Or nobody. Hell, he might not even be here."

"You'll have to talk with the girl again. Do you want me to go with you?"

"If you like. You know the folks around here better than I ever will."

91

"After lunch then. I'll find you and we can go over there together," Waters told him.

Longarm nodded. "After lunch." He grinned. "Which I expect to have just after breakfast. An' I'll have that right after I get the supper I missed last night. I just hope Miz Heinrix has plenty o' supplies in her storeroom lest I plumb clean her out."

Ben smiled. "I'll see you later, Longarm." He reined his horse and led Harry Bannister's animal around to the rear of the row of businesses on Grandview's main street, ignoring the stares of passersby who were gawking at the body draped over the saddle.

Chapter 22

Longarm returned the hammerhead to its owner at the livery stable and then had to waste a good fifteen minutes helping the man—he could not read or write so much as his own name—fill out the government voucher so he could receive payment.

"I don't like this shit," the hostler complained. "How do I know you ain't cheating me?"

"I'm a deputy United States marshal, for cryin' out loud. An' it ain't my money anyhow. What reason would I have to cheat you?"

"Well, a man never knows."

"That's the damn truth. Listen, I oughta make you feel better when I remind you that the government reimbursement rate—"

"What's that mean?"

"Reimbursement? It means to pay back. What I'm saying is the rate to pay you back for my use of the horse is double what you charge here. That ought to make you feel good about it. And just to be on the safe side, we'll ask for twice that amount. How does that sound to you? Hell, they might even go ahead an' pay the full amount instead o' chopping it back to the allowable government rate."

"Shit, you're serious?"

Longarm shrugged. "I'm not making no promises. But we'll ask for one an' hope for the other. Is that all right with you?"

"Yeah. I reckon 'tis," the man finally consented.

Longarm's belly was growling with hunger by the time he was able to stretch his legs down the street toward the café. Even so, however, he stopped in at the general store to pick up a handful of rum crooks. "I don't suppose you have anything better," he asked of the clerk who was behind the counter.

"We have a box of Hernandez y Hernandez, but they're kind of old. And they cost fifty cents apiece."

Longarm's interest perked up immediately. The Cuban-rolled Hernandez y Hernandez was one of his favorite brands. They were expensive though, and fifty cents was a bargain.

"How old?"

"Five, six years."

His enthusiasm waned. The cigars were likely dry and tasteless. Still . . . "Let me have one of those to try. And ten rum crooks."

"I have some crooks packed in apple brandy."

"Apple? I'll stick with the rum, thanks." He paid for his purchases and tucked the plump Hernandez y Hernandez into a breast pocket to enjoy after breakfast, then went on down the street to Letitia's café.

At this late morning hour there was only one other pair of customers in the place. They were dressed in suits and ties and huddled tightly together at a table in the back, paying attention to some papers laid out amid their cups and a few small plates. Longarm took a stool at the end of the counter.

"You didn't come last night," Letitia said as she poured a cup of steaming coffee for him. The aroma coming off that cup was near enough to buckle his knees.

"Me an' Ben Waters was out chasing after a fella. Turned out he wasn't the one I'm looking for. Are you mad or somethin'?" She didn't act mad, but a man never knows when or why a woman is apt to blow up and turn snorty.

"No, I'm not mad. I saw you ride in. The fellow on that horse Ben was leading . . . was he dead?"

Longarm nodded and gave her a brief account of how young Harry Bannister got that way.

"Bannister," Letitia repeated. "I think I remember him. He cowboyed for the J Z, didn't he?"

"Uh-huh."

Letitia shook her head. "It's a pity to die so young."

"Yeah, it damn sure is."

"Not to change the subject or anything, but are you hungry?"

"Right close to actual starvation, I think. Me an' Ben missed supper last night an' breakfast this mornin', an' now it's comin' lunchtime, so feed me, woman, or you might be stuck with the cost to bury me."

Letitia smiled. "I think we can take care of that." She turned away and began slicing potatoes into one skillet while a slab of steak big enough to roof a small building was sizzling in another.

When his food was cooking, she brought the coffeepot to refill his cup. She leaned close and in a low voice said, "You know, sometimes in the afternoon I close the café while I go to the store to get supplies. No one would think it odd if I pull the blinds down this afternoon and hang the Closed sign."

He smiled. "Are you suggesting what I think you are?"

"Does a chicken have lips?"

He chuckled. "No, but it has a pecker."

"Exactly." Letitia smiled. "And so do you if I remember correctly."

"After the lunch crowd has gone, you say?"

"I'll close the café and leave the back door unlocked."

"I got a call to make first, me an' Ben, then I'll come an' see what it is that you're wantin' to tell me."

"Bring your pet with you."

"What pet?" Longarm asked, puzzled by the reference.

"That one-eyed blind pet you keep in your britches, that's the pet I mean."

"I'll try an' remember to have it with me," he promised.

"Now sit back. I don't want to spill any hot grease into your lap and ruin a perfectly good afternoon."

His lunch that day was particularly enjoyable, Longarm thought.

Chapter 23

It was just after one o'clock when Custis Long and Ben
Waters rapped politely on the schoolteacher's door.
"Come," they heard from inside.

Waters removed his hat, opened the door, and
stepped inside with Longarm on his heels.

The two of them promptly tangled when Waters tried
to back out of the house, cussing under his breath, his
feet stomping on Longarm's toes. Longarm lost his bal-
ance with Ben standing on his foot and had to grab
Ben's shoulder to keep from falling. He managed to
stay upright, but for a moment it looked like both of
them would wind up in a heap on the porch floor.

"What the hell . . . ?" Longarm grumbled as he dis-
entangled himself from the town marshal.

"It's that woman. It's her, that Gloria Ames woman,"
Ben hissed. Longarm thought it a rather odd way for
Ben to put it.

"What d'you mean?"

"I mean she's in there nekkid, Longarm." The marshal was so pale Longarm thought the man might col-

lapse. And just because he saw a naked woman too. Or thought he did.

"Bullshit, Ben," Longarm shot back at him. "She can't be. She hollered we was t' come in, didn't she? You've just seen her like . . . like in a shadow or somethin' an' thought she's naked. That's all."

"Huh. Look for yourself."

Longarm did. He stepped boldly forward, grasped the doorknob, and carefully turned it. He paused and looked back at Ben Waters, then eased the door open a few inches and peeped inside.

"Shee-it!" Longarm muttered under his breath as he backed quickly out again.

"Didn't I tell you?" Ben demanded.

"Sorry I ever went an' misdoubted you, Ben."

"She's nekkid, ain't she?"

"Yeah, Ben, she's nekkid."

Gloria Ames was sprawled on the floor with a throw pillow off the couch under her neck and a cloth of some sort covering her eyes. She was not wearing a stitch of clothing. And that cloth covered *only* her eyes and forehead.

All the rest of her—all the perfectly lovely and enticing rest of her—was exposed. In full and glorious view. Lush. Soft. Damn good-looking—except for her thighs; they were a mite plump. And now both Longarm and Ben Waters knew it.

"Shee-it," Longarm repeated.

"What are we gonna do?" Ben whispered.

"I dunno about you, but I think I wanta come back some other time. God knows who or what she's expecting, Ben. But it sure as hell ain't us." The two lawmen turned tail and got the hell out of there. Pronto.

Chapter 24

"That was quick," Letitia said when Longarm showed up at the café. She poured coffee for him with professional detachment after first glancing toward the two gentlemen who were huddled over a late lunch and a stack of papers. With a sigh she added, "Not that it matters. I think Mitch and Daniel intend to be here for a while. They already told me to keep the coffee coming. That is usually a bad sign." She scowled. "Then the cheapskates will pay their ten cents for two coffees and walk out without leaving a tip. They've done this before."

"It's your table they want more than the coffee," Longarm told her. "They don't have a desk they can use for whatever it is they're doing, so they use your table instead."

"Whatever. I just wish they would go."

Longarm grinned. "They will."

Letitia went back to her washtub where she was finishing up the soiled dishware from the lunch crowd. Longarm leaned back and extended his legs. He crossed his boots at the ankles and relaxed, enjoying the contentment that comes with a full belly and a good cigar. When Letitia came back with the coffeepot several minutes later, he waved her away. "No thanks. I'm gonna go visitin'."

He stood and yawned, then ambled across the café to the table where the two businessmen sat poring over their stacks of papers. The nearer of the two looked up. "Is there something I can do for you?"

Longarm smiled at him. "No, sir, but I thank you."

The gent hitched his chair over an inch or so, putting his back squarely toward Longarm. Longarm remained standing where he was.

The other gentleman glanced up, a look of annoyance wrinkling his curly-haired good looks. This one—Longarm did not know if he was Mitch or Daniel—looked like he would have fit just fine posing as an artist's model for an advertisement for shirts. Starched shirts. He did not, however, say anything. Likely did not want to risk someone marring his complexion with a poke in the jaw, Longarm rather uncharitably decided. Still . . . drink coffee all afternoon and then not leave a tip? Shee-it.

Longarm leaned forward and began reading over the first one's right shoulder. "Oh, yeah," he said. "Metes an' bounds. You boys is dealin' with real estate, right?"

"Uh, yes. Is that all right with you, mister?"

"Please don't let me bother you none. I'm just always curious about stuff I don't already know about. An' if there is anything that I don't know about it's real estate." He leaned down and plucked a paper off the table, then another, standing back and reading them carefully.

"Here now!"

"Oh, I ain't goin' no place with 'em." Longarm's

smile was positively angelic. He even managed to make it look innocent. "I wouldn't do nothing like that."

"Put those back. Right now."

"Yes, sir." Longarm dropped the papers back where he had gotten them. And picked up several others.

The two men were passing annoyed looks back and forth between them.

"Say now," Longarm said after a moment, "is this right?"

The nearer man turned around in his chair far enough to make a swipe at the papers Longarm was holding. Longarm pulled them away at the last moment and shook his head.

"I got t' give you boys credit," Longarm said, his voice full of admiration. "Correct me if I'm wrong, but one o' you bought him some land at a dollar twenty-five an acre and the other is fixing to buy it from him at two fifty an acre so's he can sell it to some third fella for seven fifty." He whistled. "Man, that's what I call good business."

"That is what I call none of *your* business," the stuffed-shirt poster model snarled.

"Oh, I know that," Longarm said cheerfully. "An' I don't mean nothing by standing here. I'm just curious about things, that's all. Say, d'you boys mind if I set here an' see what all you're doin'? It would pleasure me ever so much if you'd let me just set quiet an' listen. But I won't say a word. Not a word. Nor ask so much as one question, no sir."

Without waiting for an answer, Longarm pulled a chair around and plunked himself down into it. He leaned forward, grinning like the village idiot, and propped his elbows on the table while he looked expectantly from one man to the other.

And sure enough, he saw what he expected. The two gents shuffled their papers together and headed for the door.

"Damn them," Letitia complained when they were gone. "Not only did they not leave a tip, they forgot to pay for their coffee." She sighed. "I won't forget to collect that dime the next time they come in though." She looked across the room at Longarm and giggled. "What did you say to them anyway?"

Longarm laughed. "Nothing really. Just tried t' be friendly."

"I'll show you friendly, mister. Why don't you leave now. Through the front door there, thank you. I'll close the café, and in five minutes you can come around through the alley. I'll leave the door open for you."

"You got you a deal there, woman." Longarm paid for his meal—and left a handsome tip, courtesy of his expense account—then headed out into the street.

Chapter 25

"What are you laughing at, you son of a bitch!" Letitia grabbed the dishcloth that had been wadded underneath her head and threw it at him. The cloth unfolded in flight and fluttered to the floor just short of his boots.

"You, uh . . . you wouldn't understand."

"No, I guess I would not." Letitia scowled and sat up, obviously intending to stand and flounce out of the room.

"The thing is . . . the thing is . . . oh, Lordy. How'm I gonna put this so's you'll understand. It's just . . . that pose . . . there's somethin' about it."

That *something* was the fact that this was the second time within a matter of minutes that he had walked into a room and found a bare-assed woman sprawled out on the floor. Except Letitia did not have her legs spread apart.

"You got nice tits, d'you know that?" he asked, going on the theory that when a conversation drifts into a danger zone, change the subject, ideally to include a compliment. The system was not foolproof but it generally worked.

"I just thought, well, you know what I thought," Letitia said.

"Yeah, an' I like that thought." He grinned. "More thrashin' room on the floor than in that narrow little bed, huh?"

Letitia ducked her head and chuckled. "Something like that, yes." She had laid a pallet of blankets on the floor and covered it with a huge, soft pink and green quilt. Longarm could not say much for those colors, but the quilt looked like it would be mighty comfortable to lie on. So did Letitia.

"Well! Are you going to just stand there or will you take your clothes off and join me?"

His grin became wider. "Now that's an invite I can't let pass by."

He laid his hat aside, unbuckled his gun belt and dropped it onto the floor at the edge of the quilt and quickly shed his boots and his clothing. It took only moments before he was standing naked in front of her.

"Come here," she said. She was still in a sitting position. She waved him close, then took hold of his leg and tugged him even closer. "There," she said when his cock was practically in her face.

She reached around behind him and ran one palm over his ass and thigh while she cupped his balls with the other hand. She leaned closer and tilted her head to one side so her forehead did not get in the way, then began to lick his balls and the base of his cock.

"Damn," he muttered. "That feels . . . that feels awful good."

Letitia mumbled something that he could not properly hear. But then she did have the excuse that her mouth was busy doing other things too.

She pulled back a bit, reached up and tugged his

cock down so she could bring it to her lips. Very slowly she peeled his foreskin back and began to suck, lightly at first and then harder, deeper.

"That feels even better'n the other," Longarm groaned.

Letitia had his balls in one hand, his ass in the other, and his cock deep in her mouth. That combination felt just fine.

After a few moments she pulled back and shook her head to get some flyaway hair out of her face. She looked up at him and smiled. "You just took a piss, didn't you?"

"Yeah. In the alley out back on my way in here."

"It tastes salty," she said.

"Oh, shit, I never thought . . ."

"No, it's all right. I said it's salty, I didn't say that I don't like it." She shrugged. "That sort of thing happens. A girl learns to expect it."

"Really? Damn!" He reached down for the washcloth, intending to wipe his pecker.

Letitia laughed. "Don't bother with that, silly. I've already washed it off." She stuck her tongue out at him to show him where.

"I'm sorry about that."

"Don't be. It sounds terrible but it doesn't taste at all bad. Oh, damn. Look there." Their conversation had taken Longarm's mind rather far from what they had been doing moments earlier, and his erection was subsiding, his cock beginning to sag and point downward as it shrank. "We are going to have to do something about that."

Letitia took his pecker into her mouth again and sucked painfully hard at first. One finger, or perhaps it was her thumb, crept beneath the crack of his butt and toyed lightly with his asshole. His cock came roaring back to full strength. After a moment she let him slip out of her mouth. She looked up at him and smiled, then lay down again on the soft and comfortable pallet.

Longarm knelt and took a moment to look her over. She was a fine-looking woman. Mature and lush and built for comfort. He could not help but make some mental comparisons between Letitia and the much younger and prettier Gloria Ames. Letitia came out just fine in that pairing, he thought. Just fine indeed.

He ran his fingertips lightly over her left tit and around the nipple, then lay down beside her.

He kissed her, a little hesitantly at first.

"Is something wrong?" she asked.

Longarm smiled. "No, darlin'. Nothin' in the world is wrong right now." And in truth it was not. He had been just a little worried that when he kissed her she might taste of urine. But she did not. Apparently her saliva had washed all that away. It was, he had to admit, a splendid way to wash one's pecker.

He kissed her again, more thoroughly this time, and his hand slipped in between her thighs to find the warm, sweet, very wet spot he was searching for.

Letitia moaned and shifted slightly on the pallet, lifting her butt and spreading her legs wide apart. "Please," she whispered into his mouth. "Please do me. Now."

Longarm said nothing. He raised himself over her and moved to position himself between her legs. Letitia reached between their bodies and took hold of his cock, guiding him in when he lowered himself onto her.

She was already wet, and he slid inside her body easily.

Letitia gasped and hitched her butt a fraction of an inch to one side, then sighed. "Hard, dear. I like it hard."

"Shh. Not this time." He began to stroke very, very slowly, very gently in and out.

"Longarm, dear. Do it hard, baby. Pound it in. Drive me into the floor."

"Shh!" He continued his slow dance, slowing even more until he was scarcely moving.

Letitia began to pump her hips, trying to pound herself against him, if clawing at his back so hard he was grateful that she had bitten her fingernails down.

"Please. Please. Pl . . . *ahhhh!*"

When she came he could feel her pussy lips quiver and clench tightly around him. She began gasping for air. "I can't . . . can't believe . . . so strong. Powerful. Damn!"

Longarm chuckled. He was still partially inside her. He lowered himself the rest of the way into Letitia's trembling body and lay there while she caught her breath. "Nice," he said.

It felt warm inside her body. Comforting. "Am I too heavy on you?"

She smiled and shook her head, stray strands of her hair tickling his chin when she did so. "You feel so very good on top of me like this. I could go to sleep with you there and sleep contented and happy."

Longarm smiled. "I'm glad you're comfortable, girl, but don't you be goin' to sleep just yet. I ain't made it yet, and you're not getting off without me having a little poke too."

"Fine." She buried her face against his neck. "Just don't be in a rush. I'm enjoying this awfully well."

"So am I, pretty girl. So am I." He lay quiet on top of her for long minutes. Then slowly, very slowly and gently at first, he began to stroke within her again. After a moment the rhythm of Letitia's breathing showed him that she had caught up with him again.

"Hard, dear," she whispered. "Do me hard."

And this time he obliged the lady.

Chapter 26

Longarm checked his Ingersoll when he emerged from the back of the café and made his way through the alley, its narrow, shadowed width strewn with broken packing crates, discarded bottles, cans, and broken bits of this and that. It smelled bad too.

He, on the other hand, smelled just fine. Letitia had insisted on drawing a basin of hot water and washing him before she let him get dressed. A man could get used to treatment like that, he figured. He idly wondered if she'd done the same for the now absent Mr. Heinrix or if this was something Letitia picked up as an inducement for her menfolk to stay close to her apron strings. It was a question he was not, however, inclined to come right out and ask, never mind how close they got for the few days he expected to be here.

Longarm paused at the mouth of the alley and pulled a rum crook from his pocket. He bit the twist off, then bent his head to light it. Old habit made him cast his eyes in both directions along the street, across the way into the alley there and up along the rooflines, checking to make sure there were no enemies visible. Not that he expected any, but then an ambush by definition is not expected. And a lawman has enemies that he does not even know about. That is just part of the nature of things, and Custis Long had been in the business long enough to know that. Long enough to survive a fair number of attempts on his life too, by damn. For him, caution had become so routine that he scarcely even realized he was doing it.

Once his cigar was properly lit and drawing well he shook out the match and flicked it away, then followed it into the street.

He walked down to the city jail and let himself in. There was a boy of nine or ten sitting behind the desk with a book in one hand and a lead pencil in the other writing down his multiplication tables. When Longarm came in, he laid his pencil down and smiled. "Yes, sir? Can I help you?"

"I was looking for the marshal. Are you his deputy?"

The kid laughed. "I'm his kid. You must be deputy marshal Long from over Denver way."

"Yes, I am, but how did you know that, son?"

"'Cause you're the only gentleman in town that I don't know. There's you and that lady that's staying with Miz Buffington. That's all the strangers that's been around lately."

Longarm grunted, then after a moment asked, "Say, how come you aren't in school, kid?"

"First, my name is Edward, but I'm called Teddy. Second, I'm not in school because we've been let out for the day."

"Is it that late already? I didn't realize."

"And in case you're wondering, I won't be in school tomorrow neither, because tomorrow in Saturday."

"Thank you, Teddy." Longarm smiled. "Truth is, I hadn't remembered that either."

"I don't guess grown-ups have to care much about such things, do you? Well, unless you're a preacher or something, that is."

"That's right, Teddy. You say Miss Ames and I are the only strangers in Grandview right now? Are you sure about that?"

"Marshal, between me and my pals, we'd know if there was anybody else. We'd know and one of us would've said something about it. We don't get so awful many strangers coming here, you know."

Longarm fingered his chin. "Yeah. Thanks. Say, Teddy, where's your dad now?"

"He's making rounds behind the stores. He'll be back soon."

"Tell me something else, please. What time does the barbershop close?"

"Oh, Mr. McPhee stays open 'til past seven weekdays. Long as he has customers on Saturdays."

"I could use a shave. When your dad gets back, would you ask him to meet me at the barbershop. If he has time, that is."

"Yes, sir, I'll tell him."

"Thanks, Teddy."

Longarm went back outside, paused for a moment to get his bearings on what was where in this town that was not his, then headed at a brisk pace for the barbershop.

He was in the middle of a trim and a shave when Ben walked in and joined him there.

Chapter 27

Lordy, a man could get used to this, Longarm thought. He felt and smelled good thanks to Letitia and a fresh application of bay rum aftershave, and he looked about as sharp as he was capable of managing with his hair and mustache neatly trimmed and his cheeks practically aglow after a close and very thorough shave. His belly was warmed by the whiskey that sat half empty before him. And he just plain felt good, all the more so after having his surplus juices drained, that service also performed by the most pleasant Letitia Heinrix. Yes, sir, life was mighty damn fine. Except for one little thing.

"So where the hell could this Blackbeard be?" he asked Ben. The town marshal was hunkered low over a mug of beer and a bowl of peanuts on the rickety barroom table. Longarm asked the question but he did not expect an answer.

Longarm tossed back the rest of his whiskey and motioned for the barkeep to bring him another, then he turned his attention back to Ben Waters. "You know what I think?" he asked.

Waters grunted and began to break open another

peanut shell, dropping the husk onto the floor when he was done. He placed the twin peanuts into his mouth and silently chewed, waiting for Longarm to continue.

"I think this Blackbeard fella ain't here at all, that's what I think."

"How'd you come to that conclusion?"

"You tell me that none o' the locals been away from home long enough or often enough to've committed kidnappings over in Nebraska an' Colorado like Blackbeard is s'posed to've done. And a little while ago your Teddy told me that there's not a single stranger in town 'cept for me an' the little lady. Young boys tend t' notice such as that, an' Grandview ain't so big as to make it hard for them. Teddy and his pals ought to know when strangers come around."

Waters grunted again, ate a peanut, and washed it down with a small sip of beer.

"D'you see what I'm sayin', Ben?"

The marshal set his mug down and paused for a moment, then asked, "So what's your conclusion?"

"I got no conclusion," Longarm told him. "Just possibilities. Could be that Blackbeard just hasn't got here yet. Could also be that Miss Ames was given wrong information. That'd be real likely if she was paying cash money for information; some son of a bitch could've made stuff up just to get a reward. Could even be, I suppose, that Blackbeard already was here an' left without finding anybody he wanted t' kidnap. There's bound to've been strangers passing through in the last few months. Maybe one o' them was this kidnapper. Maybe you an' me are wasting our time looking for him now."

"Could be," Ben agreed.

"But we can't know. Not for sure."

"No, we can't."

"I thought about just sayin' the hell with it an' goin' back to Denver empty-handed."

"But . . . ?"

"But wouldn't I feel like a prime idjit if I was t' leave town an' the next day or two somebody shows up who turns out t' be the kidnapper?"

"Yet you said yourself the information could be wrong to begin with. It could be that the real kidnapper is someplace else looking for his next victim. Could be he's never heard of Grandview, much less planned to come here."

"But how do I know, Ben? What's the best thing for me t' do if I want t' keep the peace an' enforce the law?"

"You could just sit tight and wait," Ben suggested.

Longarm sighed, then craned his neck around, searching for the bartender and that second whiskey. The man saw Longarm's annoyed reminder and this time hurried to pour a generous glass of red-eye and hustle it to the table. Longarm thanked him as politely as if he had done it right the first time.

"I think," Longarm mused, "I think this is one o' them times when I'm tempted t' pass the buck."

Ben raised an eyebrow.

"I think," Longarm said, "I'm gonna ask the boss what he thinks I oughta do."

Ben smiled. "There are times," he said, "when I wish I had someone I could ask for instruction. It must be handy."

"In this case I'm thinking that it is," Longarm admitted. "I'll get a telegram off right away."

"Not tonight you won't," Ben told him. "The office is closed now. Barry won't be back on duty until tomorrow morning."

Longarm opened his mouth to comment on the lax

qualities of any town that would allow itself to be cut off from the rest of the world come the close of business hours. Then he thought better of it. This was Ben's town and it would not be proper for him to disparage it.

"Tomorrow ought t' do," Longarm said. "Can't be anything to happen 'tween now and then."

He was wrong about that.

Chapter 28

"Marshal, sir, I got a message for you." The boy was perhaps ten or eleven years old, undoubtedly one of Teddy Waters's pals.

"All right, go ahead."

"The lady that's staying with Miss Buffington?"

"Yes, I know who you mean, son."

"Well that lady, she asked me to find you, sir, and say she'd like to see you. Are you really a U.S. marshal, sir?"

"Just the U.S. marshal's deputy. Did the lady say when she expects me to call on her?" He was thinking of his last excursion over there, when he found Gloria Ames stretched out on the floor with her wherewithal on display.

"She didn't say, sir. I think maybe right away. She paid me a whole dime to come find you. It must be real important."

Longarm smiled. "Yes, it must be." He fingered the pile of change that was lying on the table next to his whiskey glass, dragged another dime out, and gave it to the boy. "Thanks for telling me."

The kid grinned like he'd just been given a new pup, then turned and ran out of the saloon. Very likely he was not allowed inside there, either by his folks or by the saloon keeper, but who could pass up a whole twenty cents? And just for delivering a message.

"We'd best go see what she wants, Ben."

"We? You got a frog in your pocket or are you wanting me to back you with that woman again?"

"No frog. An' yes, I'd like for you t' go along."

"Fine. I'm ready whenever you are, but don't take too awful long. My missus is frying chicken tonight, and that's one of my favorites."

"Then let's go. Far be it for me to keep a man from his dinner." Longarm tossed back the rest of his whiskey and gathered his change, then dropped it into his pants pocket.

The schoolteacher's house was only a few minutes away. Longarm and Ben Waters mounted the porch, and Longarm tapped politely on the door. His knock was answered by a rather plain woman he had never met before. Actually the lady was more butt ugly than merely plain. She had mouse-brown hair pulled back in a severe bun, and there were little lines radiating out from around her mouth, which was pinched into what appeared to be a perpetual scowl. Her eyebrows met in the middle, and she looked like rouge or powder or lip color had never touched her flesh. And likely never would either. She was tall and bony and looked to be in her forties. A spinster, Longarm guessed, who never had a gentleman friend and probably did not want one, otherwise she would have been married long ago. In country like this, even as homely a woman as Miss Buffington could catch her pick of husbands if she wanted one.

Longarm briefly wondered if Miss Buffington preferred the fairer sex in her bed but as quickly put the thought aside. The truth was that he did not care either way. He was here to do a job, nothing more.

"Benjamin." The lady greeted them with a nod—but not a smile—and opened the screen door so they could enter. "And you must be the marshal from Denver."

"Yes, ma'am," Longarm said, standing with his hat in his hand.

"Please come in, both of you."

Gloria was in the parlor. She was fully dressed and sitting on a chair, not stretched out on the floor with her legs apart. She nodded a greeting when the two lawmen came in and perched rather gingerly on the sofa. "Thank you for coming."

There was the scent of cabbage in the air. Cabbage and . . . bacon? Or salt pork perhaps. Smelling it made Longarm hungry.

"The boy didn't say what you wanted to see us about," Longarm said.

"I remembered something else about the information I received. I thought it might be useful to you."

"Any help at all would be appreciated," Longarm said. "Right now we're comin' up dry."

Gloria reached for a glass on the little table at her elbow, took her time extracting a delicate little sip from it, then carefully replaced the tumbler onto the table before she spoke. "The information I was given included the name Camel. Or Campbell. I hadn't attached any importance to it and in fact forgot all about it until Miss Buffington mentioned one of her pupils whose name is Campbell. That brought it back to mind." She reached for the glass again. "I do not know what it means or indeed if it has any significance."

Longarm turned to Ben. "Does the name Campbell mean anything t' you?"

"Wilfred Campbell is a storekeeper here. He's got a wife and two boys. But Wil hasn't been away from Grandview since . . . I can't think of any time when he wasn't there in his store. Not since I've been living here. Can you, Miss Buffington?"

"No, I cannot. His sons are very good about their attendance. Not their attention, mind. Sometimes their thoughts wander, as boys are prone to do. But their physical attendance record is exemplary."

Longarm grunted.

"It probably means nothing," Ben mused out loud, "but there used to be camels in this part of the country."

Longarm gave the man a sharply questioning look.

"Surely you heard about that. It was an experiment by the army. They were looking for cavalry mounts that could chase Indians better than their grain-fed horses. They bought a small herd of camels—I don't know how many—and imported them along with some handlers who were supposed to teach the soldiers how to manage camels. The program was not a success and eventually they gave up. The camels were either sold or simply allowed to roam free."

"I reckon I did hear something about that," Longarm admitted.

"Well the way I understand it, there was one old bull that wound up living in the hills over west of town. I never saw him myself but I'm told he was a mean son of . . . uh." Waters glanced toward Miss Buffington and Miss Ames, then tried again. "I'm told he was kind of mean. He used to challenge wagons, riders, even bull trains. He'd kick, bite, make perfectly awful noises. He lived in that same area for years, then he disappeared. Everyone assumes he died of old age or a mountain lion got him. Nobody really knows."

Gloria showed some animation, sitting forward on her chair. "That is exactly what Miss Buffington was telling me," she said. "When I reacted to that name, she too remembered the old camel. And I thought . . . do you think it is possible that this kidnapper could be hiding out over there where the camel used to live? Staying along that road, perhaps, waiting for his prey to come along so he can leap out like a spider and capture the fly?"

"Anything is possible," Longarm said. He turned to Ben. "Want to take a ride with me tomorrow?"

"First light?"

Longarm shook his head. "The telegraph office is closed right now, but I'd like to get my message off to Denver before we go. It's possible someone will be in the office over the weekend, so the quicker I get that off the better."

"All right. Do whatever you need to do, Longarm, then meet me at my office. I can go whenever you're ready."

Longarm turned his attention back to the ladies. "It's too soon t' tell if this is the information we've been needin', but I intend t' check it out."

"You will let us know?" Gloria asked.

"Yes, o' course. Miss Buffington, it's a pleasure meetin' you, ma'am. Miss Ames, good evenin' to you an' thank you."

Chapter 29

NEED FURTHER INFORMATION BLACKBEARD ASAP STOP
NO SUCCESS TO DATE. Signed Long.

Longarm handed the message form to the telegrapher and signed a chit so the Department of Justice would pay for it, then he stopped in at a general mercantile and bought bacon and jerky—God knew what sort of animal the dark and stringy jerky came from—along with rice and several cans of peaches. Ben had told him the hills they would be searching were a good six-hour ride west of town. Between that and taking time to look around, they were not likely to return to Grandview until late Sunday at the earliest.

"And I'd like a handful of cigars," Longarm told the clerk who was getting his order together.

"These crooks are still the only thing I have," the man said. "Your choice, apple or rum?"

Longarm made a face. Shitty choices. But all he said was, "Rum, please." He would be pleased when he could get some of his fine-tasting cheroots again, but it looked like that would not be possible until he was back home in Denver.

The clerk finished putting Longarm's supplies into a burlap sack, rolled and tied it with twine, and presented Longarm with a bill for a dollar eighty-five. Longarm signed another chit and carried the supplies down to the livery where he had already saddled that hardheaded son of a bitch of a rental mount. Then he rode to the city jail where Ben Waters was waiting for him.

"Ready?" Ben greeted.

"Mighty near." Longarm re-tied the sack behind the cantle, narrowly escaped being kicked by Ben's horse, then had to jump out of the way to avoid the teeth of his own mount. "I hope the rest o' the day doesn't go like this," he lamented as he climbed into the saddle again and shifted his weight left and right a few times to make sure it was seated secure and comfortable on the old bastard's back. "Lead the way," he said.

The trek westward from Grandview was tedious rather than difficult. The road was well marked even if sparsely traveled. By noon they had not seen another traveler using it.

Shortly after the sun passed its zenith, they reached the ruins of a house with a tumbledown barn and partially collapsed corral nearby.

"We might as well stop here to eat," Waters suggested. "This used to be a stagecoach relay station before the railroad took over most of the passenger traffic across Nevada. Nowadays you see the occasional freight wagon come this way or some horsebackers moving through, but that's about it."

"Nothing regular?" Longarm asked.

Ben shook his head. "Nothing that I know of."

Longarm fingered his chin. He was still pondering when he swung down off his horse, sidestepped to avoid getting nipped on the shoulder, and led the animal to a

124

rusting pump that had a tightly capped can of water placed on the ground beside the pump.

"I don't know if that well is still any good or not."

Longarm looked at the gallon can of perfectly good water, then shrugged. "A man's gotta have faith," he said. He uncapped the can and dumped the contents into the top of the pump to prime it. He waited until the fluid gushed and gurgled down the well shaft, then began to work the creaky pump handle. Moments later he could feel the weight of fresh water being raised from deep underground and cold, clear water began to spew from the outflow.

"Doesn't that look good," Ben said.

While Longarm worked the pump arm, Ben watered both horses and refilled the can so future travelers could prime the pump when they needed it. Then the Grandview town marshal plunged his head neck-deep into a bucket of icy cold water. He came up sputtering and grinning. "Damn, that feels good."

Ben took over the pump handle while Longarm helped himself to a long drink and a refreshing wash, then both of them refilled their canteens.

"I don't want t' take time for a fire an' to boil coffee," Longarm said. "This water will do 'til we get where we're going."

"Fine by me," Ben said. "I'm just showing you the way."

"I don't mean t' be bossy, but . . ."

"You aren't being. Remember, I have no jurisdiction past the town limits. Out here you are in charge. I don't resent that."

"All right, Ben. Thanks."

They made a cold lunch of jerky—whatever the shit was it had a gamey flavor that Longarm did not much care for—and canned peaches, all of it washed down with more cold water from the old well. Then they tightened their cinches and headed west with the sun in their eyes.

About mid-afternoon Ben drew rein beside a weathered and sun-bleached bridge that spanned a small arroyo. A path that dipped down into the arroyo and up the other side showed that most horsemen and apparently some wagons did not trust the strength of the bridge.

Ben swung around in his saddle and indicated the surrounding country with a sweep of his arm. "Around here is where that bull camel used to come down and bother folks," he said.

"So this is where we should look," Longarm said.

"I suppose so."

"It would be nice if we could spot some smoke or tracks or some damn thing," Longarm said.

"It would be convenient," Ben said.

Longarm sat for a moment looking at the barren rock- and scrub-strewn country around them. It did not appear to offer enough sustenance for a chuckwalla to survive.

He knew better than that, of course. Even country like this had its population of bugs and birds, mice and coyotes, and badgers and big cats. But you damned sure could not tell it by looking.

"Let's step down t' stretch our legs for just a minute," Longarm said. "Then maybe we'd best split up. You take one side o' the road. I'll take the other. We'll ride off t' the side of the roadway for a couple miles then come together an' say what we've seen. If anything."

"You don't sound very hopeful."

"That's because I ain't. But we got t' look, Ben. If

126

there's any truth to this Blackbeard shit an' we can prevent a crime, well, we got t' try."

Waters nodded. "Then how's about you take this side over here, and I will look on that side. I'll see you back on the road in, oh, two hours, say."

"Fair enough," Longarm told him. "Two hours."

Chapter 30

"Ahhh!" Longarm cried out in pain.

"What happened? What's wrong, man? I didn't hear a shot."

"I wasn't shot, dammit, I was bit. This miserable son of a bitch got me right here." Longarm rubbed at his left side just above his belt. "If I hadn't been wearin' this coat he'd of tore a chunk outa me, I swear." Longarm glared at the offending mount. "I oughta send you to the knackers, you old bastard."

Ben stepped down from his horse and loosened his cinch. Longarm slipped his cinch as well but he stood as far away as possible and kept a wary eye on his mount when he did so. "Bastard," he grumbled to no one in particular.

"Did you see anything?" Waters asked.

Longarm shook his head. "Not a thing more excitin' than some snake tracks in a sandy spot. You?"

"No. Nothing."

"Doesn't mean there's nobody around, just that we ain't seen any sign of it."

"So are you ready to go back?" Waters took his canteen down and helped himself to a swallow of the now tepid water, then poured some onto his bandana and used that to cool the back of his neck.

"We've come all this way. I want t' make damn sure there's nobody out here before we give up an' go back." Longarm grinned. "I'd hate like hell t' quit now an' then find out later that we'd missed spotting ol' Blackbeard when we could've found him in his hidey-hole."

"It's your call," Ben said. "Whatever you decide, I'll back you."

Longarm peered off toward the west for a moment, then said, "We got a little more than an hour of tracking light. Let's keep on, you on your side o' the road an' me over here, for another hour. Then we'll meet down on the road again an' give some thought to laying out a camp for the night.

"It'll cost you some sleep, Ben, but I'm thinking we should take turnabout keeping watch through the night. Just in case."

"In case of what?"

"In case this kidnapper don't like anybody nosing around his lair. If he's here, he has t' be someplace that he can keep an eye on the road. That means he'd see us even if we miss seein' him. If that's so, the sensible thing would be for him t' just wait an' let us go away on our own." Longarm's grin flashed again. "But then if he was sensible, he wouldn't be goin' around kidnapping people, would he?"

"In other words, he might want to sneak down and help himself to whatever we have."

"Yup," Longarm said. "An' over our dead bodies."

"That wouldn't be friendly."

"You could almost say it'd be rude."

"One more hour, you say?"

"No point looking any longer 'n that. We'll be running out of daylight about then, and I'd like to be able to lay out our camp with a little light left in the sky."

"I know a good place where we can stop. There's a seep. At least there used to be. It always gave enough water that the stagecoaches could water their horses there."

"All right. But we'll want to approach it easy. Our friend Blackbeard could be campin' there or at the very least be getting his water there. We'd best check it for signs before we stomp around an' leave our own boot prints all over the place."

"If I remember correctly, this spring I have in mind is about a half hour ahead."

"A half hour is good enough." Longarm flipped his stirrup over the seat of his saddle and tugged his cinch tight, keeping a wary eye on the horse's teeth. He pulled the stirrup down, careful to keep it from banging into the horse's ribs, and swung lightly into the saddle. "See you then, Ben."

Chapter 31

Longarm put his best sneak on when he approached the tiny spring that drained into a natural stone basin. He took his time and crept stealthily up on . . . a half dozen quail.

The quail exploded into noisy flight when they saw him, which meant he had done a good job of creeping up on them. Had they heard him coming they would have darted into the brush and out of sight without ever leaving the ground, quail not being much for using those undersized wings without awfully good reason.

"Damn," he mumbled as he stood and stretched. Fire-roasted quail tastes almighty good and had he seen this covey in time he could have shot one or possibly two. That would have made an infinitely better supper than the jerky in his saddlebags.

He checked the area around the little spring for tracks but the only prints he found were left by birds, bobcats, and coyotes.

Once he was satisfied there had been no human visitors since the last rain—whenever the hell that was—he walked back the way he had come and reclaimed the horse he'd left tied out a good hundred yards from the water. He was leading it closer to the spring when Ben Waters came riding in.

"See anything on that side, Ben?"

Waters shook his head. "No people. No camels either. I take it you already looked around over here."

"I figure we can lay out a cold camp tonight, someplace where we can keep an eye on this spot, just in case our boy comes to water t'night," Longarm said. A cold camp made sense when man was the prey being hunted. But he would not have minded a small fire if they just had one or two of those quail to cook over it.

"Whatever you say."

"I don't have much hope of it," Longarm admitted, "but like the old maid says, slim hope is better'n none."

They filled their canteens at the spring and watered the horses, then led the animals into the brush about seventy-five yards before they pulled their saddles and spread their blankets.

The rugged, nearly barren country was silent save for the soft whisper of a night breeze and the angry yelp Longarm let out when the damned horse nipped him on the hip.

"You son of a bitch, if you was mine I'd shoot your ass an' walk back t' town."

He thought he heard Ben Waters quietly laughing, but it was too dark by then for him to see the town marshal's expression.

"Good night, Longarm."

"G'night, Ben."

They kept on searching most of the following day, neither with any real expectation that they would find anything. Which was just as well, since they could find neither man nor tracks to indicate that anyone was or recently had been in the vicinity.

They came together at the same seep late that following afternoon, riding slow and weary in the afternoon heat.

"What d'you think, Ben?"

"The same thing I thought to begin with. But now we know for sure there is no one lurking around here."

"For pretty sure, anyhow," Longarm agreed. He glanced toward the sun, which was already well on its way downhill. "It's gonna be dark long before we get back."

Waters grinned at him. "Lucky for me this old horse knows the way back to his stall. From here I can just toss the reins to him and go to sleep. He'll take me where I want to go."

"Dammit," Longarm complained. "If I tried t' do that with this misbegotten son of a bitch, I'd wake up with no kneecaps. I believe he'd bite 'em clean off."

"I agree that he'd try," Ben said.

"I'm not hearin' any sympathy from you."

"No," Waters said cheerfully. "Now shut up and let me catch up on the sleep your snoring cost me last night."

Longarm frowned. "Did I really snore?" Letitia hadn't mentioned anything about him snoring lately.

Waters threw his head back and began to howl with laughter.

"Well, did I?"

Ben laughed all the louder. But he steadfastly refused to answer Longarm's simple question even though Longarm must have asked it a dozen times more before they finally got back to Grandview well past sundown.

Chapter 32

"I guess this is where we part company," Ben said as they sat their weary horses—with equally weary men on them—at the outskirts of Grandview.

"I have a question, if you don't mind," Longarm said.

"Don't mind at all. Go ahead."

Longarm pulled a crook out of his pocket and bit the twist off but did not light the cigar immediately. It was rude, dangerous too, to smoke in a barn and certainly not something a man would do in someone else's barn. And he wanted to get rid of this mean and cantankerous horse just as quickly as he could get it back into the livery barn. "What I'm wantin' to know is if that hostler is apt t' be waitin' up for his damn horse or should I go light in case the man's asleep."

"He'll be asleep, but if I were you I would go ahead and make myself known anyway. He's been known to come out of a sound sleep with a gun in his hand, especially if he's been drinking."

"Been known to shoot when he does that?"

"From time to time he does."

"Thanks for the warning."

"Hell, I'm glad you asked. I had clean forgot about that little habit. It's been more than a year since he shot anybody."

"Shot somebody?"

"Yes, but didn't kill the fellow." Longarm could hear Ben's chuckle. "He's an awful bad shot when he's drunk. Not so good when he's stone cold sober, come to that matter."

"Jeez, you're encouraging."

Waters laughed again. "Good night, Longarm. I'll see you in the morning."

"G'night, Ben."

Longarm touched the brim of his hat, then guided the hammerheaded old SOB he was riding down the street. Letitia's window was dark and a Closed sign was propped inside the glass in the front door. She was probably asleep, he figured. It would be a shame to wake her. But on the other hand . . .

He commenced to smiling at the thought of her.

Thoughts of Letitia Heinrix kept him moving right on past the saloon, where there was still light but no noise. Apparently their business was about done for the night too. Longarm had no idea how late it was and did not want to bother striking a match so he could see the face of his watch, but he gathered that it must be pretty late.

Still, he remembered now, this was a Sunday evening. Not the busiest night for barkeepers.

He reached the livery and began humming fairly loudly in an effort to make sure he did not startle the hostler. He did *not* sing. His singing voice, he sometimes explained, was the reason he gave up cowboying and became a lawman; whenever he tried to sing the herd to sleep, he tended to spook them into a stampede instead. It was only a very small exaggeration.

The humming was not likely to carry well so he began to whistle instead. Even that came out off-key but at least it was tolerable.

He reined the horse toward the big double doors that stood gaping open to the street.

The next thing Longarm knew there was a sheet of yellow fire practically under the horse's nose.

The animal reared beneath him.

Then dropped like a hot rock.

Longarm clawed for his Colt. He got it in hand but taking time to do that meant he was still in the stirrups when the horse hit the ground, trapping his left leg under nine hundred pounds of dead weight.

He heard the ominous double click of a hammer being cocked for another shot.

Chapter 33

Another sheet of flame erupted and immediately after he heard the rain—damned hard rain at that—of lead hailstones slamming into the earth and into the body of the dying horse. The animal whinnied and tried to get up, but it was so weak it could not lift itself enough to allow Longarm to slip his leg free.

The best he could do was to raise his Colt at arm's length above his head and trigger a blind shot in the direction the shotgun blast had come from. He fired again and thumbed the hammer back for a third shot, then realized that his spare ammunition was in his coat pocket. And that was effectively trapped hard against the ground where he could not get to it without lifting his body into view. He decided not to fire that third round. He might well be needing it later.

He heard the *clunk* of a scattergun breech dropping open and some distant mumbling as the shooter pulled a pair of empty shells out and droped them on the hard ground. They made a light, ringing sound when they hit. Brass shells, Longarm realized, not the newfangled paper kind. That likely meant they were buckshot. And that most certainly meant they could fuck up a man's whole day if he got shot with one.

Longarm reached high and triggered that third shot in the direction of the reloaded shotgun.

"Damn you, you son of a bitch."

Longarm heard the drum of hoofbeats behind him, and a pistol fired.

The dull bellow of the shotgun answered the much lighter sound of the pistol.

Longarm heard a grunt and then a *thump* as his would-be rescuer came out of the saddle and hit the ground. He struggled anew to free himself from the dead horse, but his leg was held firm against the earth.

He heard heavy breathing and the sound of the shotgun breech being levered open again.

More empty shells fell with a bright, chiming tinkle. There was a moment's pause and the weapon was snapped closed again. Longarm thumbed the hammer of his Colt and waited, hoping for a chance to shoot this son of a bitch.

He heard the clatter of slamming doors and hasty footsteps as the town was brought awake by the gunfire from the livery stable. People were racing to see what the shooting was about. That was not necessarily a sensible response to gunfire but it certainly was a common one.

Under the circumstances Longarm did not object at all. He raised his torso as high as he could and fired his fourth shot.

He heard a squeal—it sounded to him like the shooter was frustrated but likely not hit—and his unknown assailant ran deeper into the barn.

Townspeople began to arrive carrying lanterns and candles burning inside hurricane lamps. Longarm shielded his eyes from the sudden brightness. "Help me get loose here."

The menfolk of Grandview ignored him, kneeling instead beside Longarm's would-be rescuer. In the light he could see now that it was Ben, who had come back to help him. Waters was bleeding from three or four wounds in his upper body and there was a deep gash in his cheek that was pouring blood.

A man Longarm recognized as the town barber took charge, peeling Ben's shirt open to expose four small and virtually bloodless wounds there. They looked like small dots of red on pale flesh. Insignificant, except where they were located, it was very likely that at least one lung was punctured and quite possibly his gut as well. If Ben had been gutshot, it could be very bad for him. Very bad indeed.

Longarm grabbed hold of someone's ankle. He was wearing unlaced shoes, his feet bare inside them.

"Hey!" the fellow protested.

"Get a couple of these men to help you lift this horse off me."

"We'll get you up, damn you, but only to put you in a cell," the man snarled.

"Hold it, Bobby. That's the U.S. marshal. Listen, mister, are you the one that shot Ben?"

"Not damn likely," Longarm answered. "Somebody was waitin' for me in the barn. Ambushed me. Ben heard an' came riding in t' help. That's when he got shot by the son of a bitch. Now *get this horse off me!*"

"Yes, sir. Jim, Ab, give me and Bobby a hand here. We gotta shift this dead horse off the marshal."

They were none too gentle about it but they did manage to lift the horse enough for Longarm to slide his leg

143

free. There was one uncomfortable moment when his spur caught on the cinch strap on his saddle, but he managed to wiggle it free and get his leg back.

"Thanks, gents."

He quickly dipped into his coat pocket—he really ought to start carrying his spare cartridges in his other pocket, he thought—and reloaded. Then he started into the dark mouth of the barn.

"Hey, where're you going, mister? Ain't you gonna help us with Ben?"

Longarm did not even break stride. He answered over his shoulder as he edged carefully into the darkness. "You boys take care o' him. I've gotta find that shooter."

Chapter 34

The barn was empty except for livestock, bedding straw, and grass hay. The shooter was gone.

Longarm ran to the big double doors at the back of the livery barn and edged over just far enough to let him see across the dim starlit corrals and feedlot. There were horses there, and mules. A few goats, he thought. But no damn human persons. No shooter.

There was little but open ground behind the livery and no alleys or other businesses built close against it—due to the smell of the stock, he assumed—but the shooter had had plenty of time to make a clean getaway while Longarm remained trapped beneath that dead horse.

The son of a bitch!

Longarm reloaded his Colt and shoved it back into its holster, took a moment to brush himself off, then went back through the barn. The front was empty except for the dead horse Longarm had been riding. He had no idea what happened to Ben Waters or his horse.

There were lights showing in the saloon now and in the barbershop. He went first to the barber's on the theory that Ben would have been taken there, but he was mistaken. The only person he saw in the shop was a thin, severe woman who was just coming out of the back when Longarm walked in. She held a porcelain teapot in one hand and a towel in the other.

"Ma'am." Longarm removed his Stetson and held it in front of his belly.

"You're that marshal from Denver, ain't you?"

"Yes'm."

"You be lookin' for my man?"

"Yes, ma'am, I am."

"Then you can do a Christian deed for me. I need this pot of boilin' water carried over to that wicked saloon place. It wouldn't be proper for me to set foot inside the devil's den. You could presarve me from that."

"I'd be glad to, ma'am. Is that where they've taken Marshal Waters?"

"Yes, 'tis. My man said he might have to operate on the gentleman, and there's better light over there or something. I wouldn't know, never having had the urge to peer inside."

"No, I can see that you wouldn't," Longarm said soothingly. The supercilious old biddy! But that part he did not speak aloud.

He put his hat back on and politely touched the brim, then took the teapot and towel from her.

The barber's wife returned to the back of the shop, chin elevated and shoulders squared, marching as stern and unbending as any soldier on parade. Lordy, but there were times that Custis Long was grateful he had no missus.

Longarm held the teapot in both hands and used the towel to fend off some of the heat from it. If the water in there was no longer boiling now that it was off the stove, it was damn close to it.

He turned half around and shouldered his way through the batwings at the saloon. At least half the grown men and a fair number of boys were gathered there.

They were not, however, lined up at the bar.

The barber—Longarm tried to remember the gent's name but drew a blank—had Ben laid out on the polished surface of the bar. The lamp wicks had all been run up high, and extra lamps had been lit and hung as well. It was as good a makeshift operating table as any and much better than most.

Ben's shirt and britches had been cut off him and a pad of bar towels were underneath his body. By the time Longarm got there his torso and abdomen had been washed with whiskey, and there was a crowd of helpers assigned to hold his arms and legs down once the "doctor" began working on him.

Longarm moved in close and asked, "Did the balls come out through his back?"

"No, dammit. I wish they had. They'll stay in there and likely fester if I can't get them out."

Longarm nodded. "You got a pick or a screwtip to draw them nigh?"

"Marshal, I've treated gunshots before. I know what I am doing." The barber sighed. He looked years older tonight than he had when he was cutting Longarm's hair. "I know that things do not look good for our friend Benjamin. The lungs could heal in time but if this one down here perforated the gut . . ." He shrugged and shook his head.

"Don't you two talk over my head, dammit," Ben muttered. "I ain't dead yet."

"Sorry."

"Ben, I got to ask you something," Longarm said.

"That you, Longarm?"

"Yeah."

"You're gonna ask did I see the son of a bitch, right?"

"That's right, Ben. Did you?"

"Just . . ." He winced and fell silent for a moment, then continued as if there had been no interruption. ". . . shadow and the flame from the shotgun blast. My horse. Is he all right?"

"He is, Ben." Longarm had no idea how the damn horse was, but the animal had not been lying dead in the street anyway. "We'll check him over when we get some better light."

"Are you all right, Longarm?"

"I'm fine, Ben, thanks. The shots all struck that horse I was on. I wasn't touched, just trapped underneath."

"That's good because I want . . . want you to find the miserable son of a bitch who did this to me. Find him and kill him, Longarm. Don't trust a jury to do it. You find him and you kill him for me. Now promise, will you?"

"I will, Ben. I promise."

The barber and the men standing close enough to hear gave Longarm some shocked looks at that, but the hell with them. If a simple thing like a promise served to ease this dying man—and Longarm was damn well convinced that Ben would not survive these wounds—then it was a good thing to say.

"You're in good hands, Ben. Now hold on, you hear? The doc has to get those balls outa you. Hold on."

The men who were charged with pinning Waters in place took hold of his arms and his legs and pressed down with all their weight while the barber took a scalpel and began cutting. Cutting and probing then cutting some more.

The blood did not much bother Longarm. He had seen an awful lot of that in his time. But when Waters began screaming for them to kill him and get it over with, Longarm slipped out into the night.

Chapter 35

•

There was someone walking the streets and alleys of Grandview, Nevada, who wanted to kill him, and Longarm had not the faintest clue as to who it might be.

The kidnapper who called himself Blackbeard? That was the obvious choice. Yet it did not make sense. He and Ben had pretty thoroughly established that none of the townspeople had been away long enough to perform one kidnapping, much less a bunch of them.

The kidnapper was *not* a local. But there was not one solitary stranger in town.

Well, apart from himself. And Gloria Ames. Both of them were trying to put a stop to the kidnappings and slap Blackbeard behind bars where he properly belonged.

Which left . . . nobody.

It wasn't "nobody" who was exercising that double-barreled shotgun though. That was not fired by some ghost of a long-dead pirate.

Come to think of it, Longarm pondered, with him and Ben having no leads to the kidnapper, it made no sense at all for the man to risk starting trouble with that shotgun. Why ambush someone who's chasing his own tail like some feist dog spinning in the dust?

Waters and Longarm were on their way back from a completely useless foray into the hills. They had nothing. They knew nothing. They were no threat to Blackbeard at all.

So why the hell would he up and risk it all by hiding there in the livery stable in ambush?

This mess, Longarm decided, was not making sense.

He walked back down to the livery, felt along the wall just inside the door until he encountered a lantern, and took it down off the nail. He lifted the globe and snapped a lucifer aflame with his thumbnail. A yellow glow spread across the alleyway that ran down the center of the barn.

Longarm adjusted the wick to produce a steady, brightly burning butterfly, then walked back outside, playing the light over the ground.

At the entrance, almost inside, he spotted the shooter's empty shells gleaming gold in the lamplight.

Longarm picked them up and carried them back inside. He replaced the lantern on its nail and examined the shells in the light. They told him little more than that they were perfectly ordinary 12-gauge shells manufactured by Union Metallic Cartridge Corporation. They could have been purchased anywhere in the United States or Canada and exhibited no indication that they might have been reloaded in the past.

"Shit!" he muttered aloud.

He carried the lantern outside again and set it on the ground so he could see to unfasten his cinch strap—he had to undo it from the wrong side because the dead horse, which was already cold to the touch, was lying on it—and tug his saddle off the animal. He removed both

152

saddle and bridle and carried them and the lantern inside the barn.

He draped his gear over the wall of an empty stall and, lighting his way with the lantern, went to the tack room that doubled as sleeping quarters for the hostler.

That worthy gentleman was passed out on the floor beside his bunk, an empty whiskey bottle in one hand and his dick in the other, his fly unbuttoned and his britches pulled down over his hips. Longarm could not decide if the man had been trying to get his pants off so he could go to bed or if he merely wanted to pull his pecker out so he could take a piss. He had not made it onto the bed, which was probably just as well because he had managed to piss all over himself. The tack room stank of urine and tobacco juice.

Longarm shook his head. There would be no point in trying to get any information out of the hostler. Not tonight anyway.

Longarm backed out of the foul-smelling room and returned the lantern to its nail before again lifting the globe, this time so he could blow out the flame.

"Damn," he complained to himself as he headed back toward the saloon.

Chapter 36

At four seventeen in the morning, with the eastern sky beginning the process of turning gray, Grandview Marshal Benjamin Waters steeled himself against the pain and smiled when he asked his wife and son to go home and get some sleep.

"It's better now. I'll be fine until you get back."

"I don't know. . . ."

"Please."

Longarm was standing nearby. He could see from the tension in Ben's body how much this effort was costing him. The currency was pain and his bill was large. "Miz Waters," he said, stepping forward to touch her elbow and steer her away from the bar where her husband still lay, "I reckon it'd be a good notion for you t' do what Ben asks." He smiled, first at her and the boy, then at Ben.

Waters nodded briefly, then closed his eyes as another jolt of agony ripped through him. Longarm could not begin to imagine the pain Ben was forcing himself to endure so as not to alarm his wife.

"Please, ma'am. You an' the boy do what he says. If

155

there's any change, we can come fetch you," Longarm said.

"If you're sure. . . ."

"The onliest thing we can be sure of," Longarm said, "is that we'll get you if you're needed."

"You can count on that," one of the men in the crowd said. The room was nearly full. Someone had opened the doors and every window in the place, but it was stuffy and smelled of tobacco and sweat.

"Please, Marta," Ben very quietly put in. "Please."

"Well . . . if you say so."

"I do."

She smiled. "You have uttered those words before, Benjamin Waters."

"And I would gladly say them again. You are a good woman, Marta. Thank you for sharing your life with me."

"Don't talk like that, Benjamin. You sound so . . . final."

Ben smiled. "We can talk more later."

"Yes," she said. "Later."

"Longarm, would you escort Marta home? It must be late and I would not want harm to come to them."

"I'd be proud to, Ben." Longarm offered his elbow. The lady hesitated for a moment, then took it. She motioned to the boy. "Come along, Tadpole. We'll come back in the morning."

The boy colored, obviously distressed that his private family nickname had been put on public display, but he leaned over and gave his dad a kiss on the forehead, bringing a smile to Ben's gray and haggard face, then turned and started for the door.

Mrs. Waters paused, obviously uncomfortable about showing emotion in front of the entire town, then she too kissed Ben. The marshal's lips were stained with frothy blood but she bent down and kissed him most tenderly on the lips. She touched his hands and whispered something that was private between the two of them, then she too turned to leave.

Longarm escorted her out into the clean chill of the morning air.

They were perhaps halfway from the saloon to the marshal's home when Longarm heard a dull, muffled gunshot.

"What was that?"

Longarm suspected that he knew what it was but all he said was, "I'll find out direc'ly, ma'am. If it's anything you or the boy is needin' t' know, I'll carry the word to you."

"Thank you, Mr. Long. You are very kind."

Longarm got the story when he returned to the saloon. Once his wife and son were gone so they would not see what he intended, Ben plucked a revolver out of the holster of someone standing close by and, moving swiftly, cocked the pistol, pressed the muzzle tight against his right temple, and pulled the trigger.

"He made a helluva mess," the saloon keeper complained.

"It'll clean up," Longarm said, his steely expression making it very clear that any more such talk would not be appreciated.

"The bullet broke one of my finest bottles of spirits," the man persisted.

Longarm's lips thinned but he was *not* smiling. "Tell you what, friend. Just add some more creek water to your stock. An' by the way, as a federal officer I'm thinkin' to go through that stock o' whiskey an' see that the tax stamps on every one o' them are in order."

The phony smile became broader. "Either that,"

Longarm said, "or you can shut your mouth now. A good man died here t'night. He don't need the likes o' you hanging aroun' over his dead body like a vulture settin' in a tree. D'you understand me?"

"Uh . . . yes, sir. Perfectly."

"Then you an' me got no problem," Longarm said. He reached for a rum crook, took out his pocketknife, and very slowly and carefully trimmed the twist off. He dropped the twist into a nearby spittoon and chewed the cigar for a moment. The saloon keeper was quick to strike a match and hold it so Longarm could get his smoke lit.

"Thank you kindly, neighbor," Longarm said, his voice mild.

Longarm turned and walked out into the street. There were plenty of others there who could help with Ben Waters's mortal remains.

But the question remained: Who the hell fired those shots? And what did that have to do with a kidnapper who called himself Blackbeard?

Chapter 37

Longarm was tired. He had been up all night with the vigil for Waters, he and nearly every other male in the town. Too much whiskey and too many cigars during that time had left his mouth tasting like a goat had come along and crapped in it.

He noticed with some relief that there was a lamp burning behind the drawn blinds at Letitia's café. None of the decent women of the community had been in the saloon overnight, but they may well have held prayer sessions through the night. And now Letitia was preparing for an early breakfast crowd.

Longarm tapped on the glass until she came to the door and peeped out. When she saw who it was she quickly opened the door, let him inside, and pushed it closed again. She threw herself onto his chest and held him close.

"Are you all right, Custis?"

"Yeah, but Ben is dead."

"Oh, dear. Is Marta all right?"

"She will be. But not for a while, her nor the children."

Letitia stepped back, her hands knotting and twisting

a dish towel. "The poor thing. I need to send something. A pie. I can take a pie. And a ham. Some candied yams. Oh, dear, I just can't think."

"You're doin' fine," Longarm said. "D'you got any coffee?"

"Yes, of course. Sit down. No, over there at the counter if you don't mind. I want you close. Just sit. I will bring your coffee."

Longarm nodded and sat where she indicated. He squeezed his eyes tightly shut and rotated his head to loosen his rigid neck and shoulder muscles. He had not realized just how tired he was until he was sitting there with his eyes closed. It was tempting just to go to sleep, right there on the lunch counter stool.

The scent of coffee roused him. When he opened his eyes, there was a steaming cup of freshly brewed coffee sitting in front of him.

"Thanks."

Letitia smiled. "I put that there five minutes ago."

"Par'n me?"

She nodded. "It's true. Five minutes at least." Letitia laughed. "You were snoring at the time."

"Damn."

"Drink that, then why don't you slip into the back room before I open the place for business. You can get some sleep. Lord knows you need it."

"Someone is tryin' t' kill me, Letitia, an' I don't know who or why. He's the one that killed Ben, though it was for sure me that he was layin' in wait for last night."

"He will still be here when you wake up. You can hunt him down then. Or wait for him to hunt you if he wants you all that badly. Now go. You look terrible. You need some sleep."

Longarm took a long swallow of the coffee, then abruptly nodded. Letitia was right. He did indeed need sleep.

And the bastard with the shotgun would still be there later.

Longarm took a few minutes to finish the coffee—the cigar he'd been smoking had long since gone out while he dozed—then kissed Letitia and went into the back to stretch out on her narrow bed.

He did not think he had ever before felt anything as good as that mattress. Well, hardly anything.

When Longarm woke up some hours later, he let himself out into the alley behind the café and made his way around to the street entrance again. This time it was standing open and there were half a dozen—no, seven actually—townspeople inside.

"What's for breakfast today?" he asked. A couple of the men who were sitting nearby gave him an odd look.

Letitia struggled to suppress a smile. "It's lunchtime, which you obviously do not know."

"For me it'll be breakfast, ma'am. Would it still be possible t' get some?"

"Yes, of course."

"That's what I'd like then. Eggs, biscuits with gravy, maybe a nice steak t' go with those. Can you do that?"

"Take a seat. I will bring them to you when they are ready."

He chose a chair that would keep his back to the wall, then leaned back and crossed his ankles. He felt a hell of a lot better after getting some sleep. Now all he needed was a good, big breakfast—which Letitia was about to serve him—and a shave. He ran his fingertips over his cheeks. The stubble was bristly and sharp.

Yeah, he needed a shave bad. He had not had an opportunity to get rid of those whiskers since the morning he and Ben had set out in search of the falsely rumored stranger out in the camel's hills.

Just as soon as he was done with his meal, whatever anyone wanted to call it, he would have to get that shave and maybe pick up some gossip when he did so.

But in the meantime . . .

Letitia set not a plate but an entire platter before him, the smell of it causing Longarm's mouth to run water in anticipation.

Chapter 38

Longarm felt like a new man when he walked out of the café, his belly full and a cigar between his teeth. He tilted his hat against the morn—no, the afternoon sunlight—and headed for the barbershop to get that long overdue shave.

"Haircut for you today, Marshal?" The barber was busy with one man already in his chair and another was waiting.

"No, thanks, Doc. Just the shave."

"Take a seat. It won't be long." The man was true to his word. He finished shaving around the ears and on the back of the neck of the man in his chair and made quick work of a trim for a gentleman who certainly looked the part of a banker whether he was one or not. Whoever and whatever he was, Longarm had not seen him before.

When it was Longarm's turn in the chair he stretched his legs out and opened his shirt so the barber could take the collar off. "This thing is getting rumpled. Would you like for me to put a new collar on when I'm done with your shave? First quality celluloid, very crisp and fresh and it should stay that way mighty well."

"How much?"

"Another two bits."

"All right I can go that much."

The barber flapped his sheet with the dexterity of long practice and it floated on a cushion of air to settle lightly over Longarm from his throat to his knees.

Longarm rather enjoyed the ritual of a barbershop shave. The sound of the brush whipping up lather. The slap and slide of the razor being sharpened on a leather strop. The buzz of conversation and rustle of newspapers among men waiting their turns in the chair.

Not that there were others in the shop at this late hour. Longarm seemed to be the last customer in the place.

The barber made short work of applying lather. While he worked, he talked. "Have you caught the man who murdered Ben?"

Longarm did not shake his head. By then there was a razor pressed against his throat. "No, not yet."

"But you will?"

"Damn right, I will," Longarm declared. "Your marshal was a decent man. His murder can't go unpunished."

The razor blade was feather light as it sliced his accumulation of whiskers away.

"Do you want me to trim that mustache?"

"No, reckon I'll do that later myself."

The man left Longarm's mustache alone, but he did bring out his scissors to trim Longarm's nose hairs and inside his ears. "Almost done," he said.

A small bell over the door tinkled brightly, and a young man—a very young fellow, actually—came in.

"Hello, Bobby. You aren't needing a trim already,

surely. I just did you the other day." The barber chuckled. "And you're several years away from needing a shave."

Bobby scowled, obviously in no mood for humor today. "Move aside, sir."

"What?"

"Please move. I don't want to hurt you by accident like I did Mr. Waters."

The kid—he looked to be no more than sixteen if he was that old—opened his coat and brought out the stubby sawed-off shotgun he had been concealing there.

A sawed-off 12-gauge is one formidable son of a bitch, Longarm thought, not for the first time.

Not at all the sort of thing a man likes to face when he is sitting peacefully in a barber's chair. Or for that matter at any other time as well.

Bobby thumbed back the hammers on the double gun and pointed it toward Longarm and the town barber.

"Please move now."

It was Longarm who moved first.

Chapter 39

Longarm triggered the Colt that he was holding in his lap beneath the barber's sheet.

The sheet billowed outward, the cloth containing the smoke at least for the moment.

The casually aimed bullet spat outward as well. It struck the kid in the belly, doubling him over. "Oof!" His eyes went wide and he dropped into a sitting position on the floor, surrounded by the bits of hair from an entire day of haircut customers.

Longarm threw the sheet aside. The flame from his pistol shot had set it afire.

The barber yelped and began stomping on his sheet, trying to put out the fire before the whole place went up.

Longarm's concern was the double-barreled 12-gauge that the kid still held slanting across his chest.

"Drop it, boy!" Longarm's voice was harsh, hard, and freezing cold. Even so Bobby ignored him, mouth gaping in disbelief at the fact that he had been shot and very likely mortally wounded. "Drop it. I ain't gonna tell you again."

Bobby still clung to his shotgun.

Longarm took aim and put a bullet dead center into the kid's forehead.

His head snapped backward and the back of his head exploded, spraying the shop floor and lower wall with blood and brain tissue. In death his hand clenched hard enough to trip one of the shotgun triggers. A rain of heavy buckshot shattered the shop window and went flying off across the street.

A man who had been walking past rushed to the door and screamed, "Christ, man, what are you doing in here? You like to killed me. . . ." When he saw what was left of Bobby stretched out on the floor, he clamped his mouth shut. "Oh, uh . . . sorry. I, uh . . . I'd best go tell the marshal. No, wait, the marshal is dead, isn't he. Jesus! What is going on around here? We never had no trouble before. Who is that anyway? I can see him but I sure as hell can't figure out who he is."

"It's Bobby," the barber said as he finished his little fandango on the still smoldering sheet. "Bobby Templeton."

"Jesus. No! That kid?" The man looked at Longarm, then blanched at the sight of the tall lawman who still had his big Colt in hand. "I, uh, I ain't, questioning you, Marshal. No sir, I ain't."

Longarm ignored the man and turned to the barber. "You knew the boy. Any idea what might have set him off? He's the one tried to gun me down last night an' ended up killing Ben Waters by mistake."

"Why would Bobby do that?"

"Damn if I know but it has to've been him. Who is he? Who *was* he, I mean."

The barber slumped into his own chair, obviously shaken by what had just happened in his little shop.

"Bobby is . . . was . . . fifteen, I think. Maybe sixteen. Still in school anyhow. His pap runs the saddlery down the street. Does all sorts of leatherwork. Builds saddles and repairs harnesses and shoes and the like. Anything with leather, Bill Templeton can do it. He's a magician with leather. His boy . . . long as I can remember Bobby has helped his dad around the shop. The kid could plait a rawhide lariat by the time he was eleven or twelve years old. He loved to make them. I think all the cowboys and half the businessmen in town have one of his lariats. I know I have one myself. Have it on the wall in my living quarters back there. He didn't sell it to me either. It was a gift. He said . . . said it was for all the candy I used to slip to him, gumdrops out of the jar that I keep for the little kids to hush them up while I cut their hair. Bobby is . . . Bobby was a real good kid himself, Marshal. Real good."

"Until he decided to gun down a deputy United States marshal," Longarm said in a dry voice.

"Yeah. Until then."

"Any idea why he would want so bad to shoot me?"

The man shook his head. He was speaking to Longarm, but he kept staring at the gore that was spreading across his floor. It would take an awful lot of scrubbing to get rid of all that. "No, sir. I got no idea why anybody would want to do that. You haven't done nothing to aggravate folks since you come here. Not that I've heard anyway, and I hear pretty much everything that any human being in this town says or thinks or wants. A barber hears it all, you know. I never heard anything against you. Not anything."

"All right. Thanks."

Longarm was in the middle of the next block before he remembered that in all that excitement he had forgotten to pay for his shave and the new celluloid collar.

Later, he thought. He would stop in later and pay.

Not that he expected to be welcomed back into that particular shop, not after the mess he had made there.

He wondered if Bobby Templeton's father was of a vengeful nature. If so, he probably should find the saddlery and work things out between them right now. On the other hand, he had no desire to be the one to tell a father that his son was dead.

Perhaps it would be better if he let things be. If Templeton wanted him for anything, he would be easy enough to find—the only stranger in town.

Chapter 40

Longarm walked back down to the livery. The hostler was bleary-eyed but upright. He looked like he had one helluva hangover though. But then he deserved one if he had finished that bottle all by himself.

"You here for a horse?" the hostler asked when he saw Longarm approach. The dead horse had been hauled away by someone.

Longarm shook his head. "That ain't what I came for."

"Oh." He winced. "Then you wanta know what happened, don't you?" the man mumbled.

"That's right," Longarm said.

"It was Bill Templeton's kid Bobby that gave me the bottle. I dunno where he got it, but he just came up and gave it to me. Didn't say nothing, just handed me the bottle and left. I didn't mean to do nothing wrong by drinking it."

"You didn't do anything wrong," Longarm told him.

"Glad you feel that way about it."

"About your horse, you can submit that voucher I gave you and demand repayment for the loss of your an-

171

imal. I'll see to it that our clerk honors the request. You'll be paid to cover your loss."

"That son of a bitch wasn't worth much."

"No," Longarm said with a grin. "He wasn't."

"You ain't mad at me for what happened?"

"It wasn't your fault," Longarm assured him. "Anyway, the boy is dead now."

"He tried for you again?"

"Yeah, I'm afraid he did."

"Now why in hell would a nice kid like that try and shoot somebody?"

"That's what I was hoping you could tell me," Longarm said. "Last night, when he came by and gave you the bottle, did he say anything? Do anything that would help tell me why?"

"Not that I can think of. They said he had a shotgun that he used to shoot Ben with, but I never saw it. He came in . . . kids do that sometimes, you see . . . they come in and look at the horses. Feed them. Pet them. Sometimes they sweep up for me in exchange for letting them take a horse out for an hour or two. The town boys, that is. They have pals on the ranches who ride in to school every day and sometimes the town boys like to be able to ride out away from the eyes of their folks. Go out somewhere and swim naked in a creek or sit in the shade and smoke. Boys always want to do things without their parents knowing. That's part of growing up."

Longarm nodded. "Ain't it just."

"Bobby wasn't different from any other kid when it came to things like that. But he was never mean and I don't know of him ever causing trouble for anybody."

Longarm sighed. "There has t' be a reason. I just wisht I knew what it was."

"I'm sorry I can't help you, Marshal. If I could I

surely would. As it is I feel responsible for what happened here. If I hadn't got drunk . . ."

"What happened, happened, that's all. You didn't do anything wrong."

"Glad you feel that way about it. But I'll always wonder if Ben would still be alive today if I hadn't drunk so damn much."

That was a burden the man would have to carry by himself, Longarm knew. It was one no one of this earth could help him with. "Thanks for your help. If you remember anything else . . ."

"I'll sure let you know," the hostler promised.

Longarm walked back the way he'd just come.

"Marshal!" a voice called loudly from behind him.

Longarm, his nerves on edge after being assaulted twice in one day, grabbed his Colt and whirled around.

Chapter 41

"No. Please!" The kid threw his hands up to cover his face as if afraid to see what happened next. A dark, damp stain began to spread across the front of his corduroy britches, starting at the crotch and running down his left leg.

Longarm stopped himself from bringing the trigger the rest of the way back. He hastily shoved the revolver back into its holster. "Jeez, kid, I'm sorry. I'm on edge. A little."

"Y-yes, sir."

Longarm recognized the boy as the helper who sometimes delivered telegrams for the operator.

"This came in a, a little while ago, sir. I brought it as quick as I could, but I didn't know where you was." He very carefully held out a slightly crumpled yellow envelope and edged forward one sliding half-step at a time until he was close enough to lean in the rest of the way and deliver the flimsy.

"Thank you, son." Longarm reached into his pocket for a tip—he figured he owed the boy a good one after the fright he must have given him—but when he looked up again the boy was gone. "Scared the piss outa him," Longarm muttered under his breath while he used his thumb to slit the envelope open.

BLACKBEARD COMMA AMERICAN COLONIST PIRATE KILLED 1718 BY BRITISH NAVY STOP WHY DO YOU NEED TO KNOW QUERY. Signed: Vail.

"That's it?" Longarm roared aloud. "That is fucking *all* they tell me? I already knew that much."

He read the telegram again, but the words on the paper did not change. There was nothing, not a hint in there about a kidnapper who called himself Blackbeard.

"This is no damn help," he grumbled, wadding the message into a ball and flinging it aside.

He strode off and had gone a good city block when he suddenly stopped, turned around, and lengthened his stride all the more. When he got back to the spot where he had tossed the telegram down, he had to look around for it; the wind had blown it to the side of the street. He spotted it lying against the sidewalk in front of a hatter's shop.

Longarm retrieved the telegram form and smoothed it out as best he could, then folded it carefully and put it away in a coat pocket.

That telegram, he realized, told him a hell of a lot more than he thought at first reading. Or second. In fact, it told him quite a lot.

He turned and set off once again but in a slightly different direction this time.

"But that is terrible," Gloria Ames said, one delicate hand at her pale and lovely throat. "You say he was just a boy?"

Longarm nodded. "Just a kid. Everybody says he was never in no trouble before now. Nobody has any notion why he up an' killed the marshal an' tried to murder me."

"He must have been the kidnapper," the pretty girl ventured.

"You might think so," Longarm said, "'cept the boy was never away from home. Not even t' spend the night with a pal much less t' be kidnapping innocents all the way back in Nebraska or Illinois or wherever."

"Nebraska," Gloria said. "In our case, I mean."

"Right. Anyway, the Templeton boy couldn't've been this Blackbeard fella. I'm sure of that."

"One hopes, you know. Hopes for justice to be done."

"Yes, ma'am."

"What will you do now, Marshal?"

"Reckon there isn't much left 'cept to go back t' Denver an' see what the boss wants me t' do next."

"Yes, that makes sense." Gloria picked up her handbag and reached inside. She was smiling. "You at least should be compensated for your trouble. I know you tried diligently."

"I don't need no rewards. Especially since I didn't accomplish nothin'," he said. "But I'll stay on the case as much as I can. You can count on that."

"Very well, I . . . oh, hello, Miss Buffington." Gloria withdrew her hand from her handbag and smiled at the schoolteacher. "I did not realize it was so late."

"I let the children go home early today," the older lady said. She looked very tired. "One of my children was murdered today, you know." If looks could kill, Custis Long would be a dead man under the teacher's unforgiving gaze.

"Shot, ma'am, not murdered. Shot after he done murder himself. He's the one as killed Marshal Ben Waters. He's the one tried twice t' kill me."

177

Miss Buffington sniffed.

"Who was it?" Gloria asked.

"Bobby Templeton, that is who."

The younger girl shook her head. "I am afraid I don't know him."

Miss Buffington snorted. "I would say that you should. You spent the entire afternoon at the church picnic yesterday fluttering over him. And don't you think I didn't see. If the child had been a few years older, I would have thought you were . . . well, never mind what I might have thought, that's all. Never you mind."

"All afternoon?" Longarm asked.

"Yes, indeed. I saw that much with my own eyes. Lord knows what happened later. I came home. Miss Ames here, who will be leaving my home as soon as she can pack her things, said something about staying for evening services. But just this afternoon on my way home I learned there was no evening service last night. The pastor was called away to minister to a dying parishioner. Miss Ames did not return from services until hours after dark. Nine, perhaps as late as ten o'clock."

"That's interesting," Longarm said. He looked at Gloria Ames. "D'you want me t' walk you over to the stage station? Or will you be stayin' on, takin' a room at the hotel maybe."

"Oh, I believe I shall be leaving now, just as Miss Buffington suggests."

"Yeah, I reckon that sounds real sensible," Longarm said dryly. "Then I'll meet you at the stage station. We can ride east t'gether."

"Thank you, Marshal. You are a gentleman, sir."

"Not really," Longarm told her.

He left the girl to her packing and went to tell Letitia Heinrix good-bye. He had few good memories of Grandview, but that sweet lady was responsible for near about all of the ones he did have.

Chapter 42

Miss Ames was dressed for travel in a sturdy gown and duster. She struggled to handle her handbag, an umbrella, and a rather large portmanteau all at the same time. Her hat, a rather battered and tatty thing, was tied in place with a silk scarf. Somehow she managed to look delicate and rather pretty.

"Miss," Longarm said, dipping his head and touching the brim of his Stetson, "ready for our trip?"

"I am, sir."

Longarm reached inside his coat and produced another of the dark and knobby rum crooks. Lordy, he would be glad to get back to Denver where he could get some more of his beloved cheroots.

"I would prefer that you not smoke in my presence," the young woman instructed, her manner haughty and her expression stern.

"I don't much give a shit what you prefer," Longarm told her.

"Sir, I insist—"

"Shut the fuck up," Longarm snapped.

Gloria's mouth gaped like a fish sucking air.

"An' I'll take that bag if you don't mind," he added. He reached out and plucked the handbag away from her before Gloria realized what he was up to.

"You was reaching in there a while ago. Figured to shoot me, didn't you? Had some sort o' little hideout gun and you was gonna shoot me, then make up some yarn about me assaulting you or some such shit as that."

While he spoke, Longarm dug through the bits and pieces of this and that that he found inside Gloria's bag.

"What's this?" he said, fishing out a box of lambskins and holding them up. "So much for bein' a virgin. Who an' what are you, anyhow? I know you're no innocent young girl from Nebraska an' likely you never had a brother. So who the hell are you?"

"What are you looking for in there?" the girl snapped, her voice assertive now and harsh.

"Figure you t' have a gun in here."

"But you don't find one."

"No, I don't find one."

"That is because," she said, "it is here." She pulled her hands out of the pockets of her duster. In her right hand she gripped a small but lethal nickel-plated revolver, a little Smith and Wesson breaktop or one of the imitators.

"You fixin' to shoot me, are you?"

Her chin came up and there was fire in her eyes. "I am, damn you."

"Mind if I ask why?"

"My name is Gloria Benton. Does the name mean anything to you, you bastard?"

"Benton. Same as the pair of idiot brothers I had t' shoot here a little while back?"

"The very same."

"So when you heard I shot those fool boys, you decided t' come gunnin' for me yourself," he said.

"Our father would have done it, but he is in prison on a trumped-up charge."

"Seems a pity you ain't in prison too. But don't worry. We can correct that little oversight," Longarm said.

"Someone will have to catch me first, and that may not be so easy." She smiled and said, "A girl like me knows how to avoid John Law."

"You wasn't able to avoid me."

"But I came looking for you, didn't I? And now I shall kill you and be done with it. This is for Tommy."

Gloria Benton raised the little revolver and pointed it at Longarm. Her finger dragged back on the trigger and the hammer began to slowly rise.

She was a girl, a pretty girl at that, but she had chosen to play a man's game, and she was not nearly good enough at it to best the likes of Longarm.

Before she could overcome the very heavy trigger pull those little double-action pocket guns had, Longarm's Colt was in his fist.

His hand was quick and his aim deadly.

Longarm's first shot struck Gloria low on the right breast. It broke a rib and pierced her lung and burst out again through the soft flesh of her back.

The girl's hand involuntarily jerked in response. The little .32 fired, and her bullet flew somewhere high overhead.

"Drop it," Longarm ordered. She still had the pistol in her hand and she still was capable of using it.

Gloria struggled to take aim at him. Again she tried to overcome the stiff resistance of the heavy trigger pull. The muzzle of the pistol wavered back and forth even as she dropped to her knees.

"Fuck it," Longarm muttered.

He put a bullet into her left eye and the once-pretty girl's head changed shape as it tried to explode outward.

Longarm looked around. The people who had been on the street moments earlier were all gone now, disappeared indoors. He did not blame them.

He carefully reloaded his revolver and returned it to the leather, then stepped forward. He bent down and tugged the hem of Gloria's gown down so her limbs were not exposed. Not that it mattered now, of course.

Then he stepped back and checked his Ingersoll.

The damn stagecoach was running late.

Watch for

**LONGARM AND THE
HELL RIDERS**

the 345th novel in the exciting LONGARM
series from Jove

Coming in August!

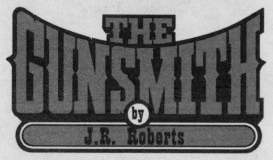